LAILA

Translated from the Arabic by Hajer Almosleh

By Fadi Zaghmout

REBEL SATORI PRESS

New Orleans & New York

Published in the United States of America by
Rebel Satori Press
www.rebelsatoripress.com

Originally published in Arabic by Kotob Khan, Cairo. English
translation first published by Signal 8 Press.

Cover image: Manuela de Gioia
Art direction: Cristian Checcanin

ISBN: 978-1-60864-375-2
eISBN: 978-1-60864-376-9

Laila – Fadi Zaghmout
Table of Contents

DEDICATION

To the Arab women who fight for equal rights,

stand up for their truths, and refuse to abide by

society's lies.

THE MOMENT OF MY DEPARTURE

Fate surpassed all expectations it might have had of its own arbitrariness the night I departed this world. It came out of the blue as Tariq and I indulgently messed about in my bedroom. Suddenly and unexpectedly, it came, the way it had twenty-eight years ago on the long-awaited night of my birth, the night my mother's abdomen convulsed with labor, announcing my arrival to the world.

My mother's screams as she tensed her thigh muscles and pushed me out were echoed years later by Tariq's moans and groans as he tensed his thigh muscles while I slipped in and out of him the very second I died.

I was about to climax, mounting him from behind, a dildo strapped to my crotch. He lay naked on his stomach, his hands and feet tied with ropes to the four bedposts. I grabbed his soft hair as I inserted the dildo into him, drunk on a feminine power so absolute, establishing my irrevocable domination of him. Like my mother in labor on my aunt's wedding night, Tariq's screams echoed in the room. His ecstatic groans were a mixture of his delicious pain and our erotic thrill. And just like my mother, Tariq was captive to the pain of a single act which completely changed his life in a way he never expected.

Two moments marked my beginning and my end: the first, my birth, a turning point in my mother's life. The second, my departure, a defining and unforgettable moment poised to haunt Tariq for the rest of his life. In the first, my screams filled the room as I gasped for my first breath of air. In the second, echoes of my hysterical laughter reverberated across the room as I saw the confusion on Tariq's petrified face when had realized that my limp body, slumped on his bare back, was not merely out of exhaustion after my surging climax. Tariq realized that my body, drained as it was of the life that had coursed through its veins until then, would never stir again.

CHAPTER 1

DON'T BEMOAN THE TREACHERY OF TIME

TARIQ

WHENEVER I pictured death, my mind never moved past the moment my soul left my body. I often wished my soul would be gently withdrawn, taking me with it like an old woman drifting to eternal sleep on her own bed, surrounded by her children and grandchildren. Yet, I could never shake the feeling that I would most certainly die in a horrible car crash caused by my own reckless driving.

Except that death had a different plan for me. It didn't come the way I had pictured and expected. Fate had dictated that the manner of my death would exceed all my expectations. Death opted for a sudden, horrifying end, imbued with a peculiar flavor. Had I been the one writing my own mortifying end, I wouldn't have been able to envision it the way it actually unraveled, nor would I have been able to predict the chain of events which ultimately followed. Had I known that the dead lingered to watch life unfold on earth after they drew their last breath, I wouldn't have chosen to leave at that particular moment. I would have clung to life and tried to change its course.

I had always loved to hum celebrated verses, lines from poems capturing the treacherous nature of human relationships. But I never anticipated that those same words would accompany me the moment I stopped existing. Neither did I imagine feeling my mouth repeat them while my tongue lay still, motionless, as my soul, light as an exhale, was yanked out of my body and left to levitate and hover around the room.

I watched Tariq tear my body up after he tore himself free
from the binding ropes and pushed me off him. I watched him
check my pulse. Watched him realize I was gone for good.

Up against the ceiling, I hummed seductively the way I
did in the past to tantalize Tariq when we role played during
sex.

'Don't bemoan the treachery of time,
Dogs have often danced on the cadavers of lions.
Their dance doesn't make them superior to their masters,
Lions will always be lions. Dogs just dogs.'

I tried to convey these lines to him, repeating them over
and over again like a desperate incantation, hoping he would
hear me. I was suddenly overcome by fear: what if there was
hope, a slim chance of me returning to my body, a chance
which Tariq was now busy decimating, leaving me shackled
in this space?

I wanted to bounce on him, ride his soul the way I had
ridden his body earlier, but I soon discovered that having
left my body did not necessarily entail acquiring the power
to transmigrate to the bodies of others. A strange conviction
swept over me at the same time, a certainty that what was
done was done. All that was left for me now was to watch
the story unfold after my death, just as I had watched it and
experienced it while I was alive.

Still, I carried on screaming into the void, hoping Tariq
might somehow hear me. 'What are you doing? You maniac!
What the hell are you doing?' My screams fell on deaf ears.
I changed my tone. It became softer. Calmer. I hoped that
a gentler vocal pitch would succeed to infiltrate the air
enveloping both my soul and his body. 'Tariq, honey, why don't
you take a deep breath and think this over? You're going to get
in some serious trouble for this.' But he didn't respond. He

left me feeling helpless, gutted, completely powerless, trying to locate my own hands to slap my face in disbelief at the atrocity of what was happening in front of me.

I fell quiet for a moment, but I couldn't remain silent seeing how he was dismembering my body. I tried to appeal to him.

'Why are you doing this?'

'Are you scared?'

'Have you lost your mind?'

'Why are you being a jerk?'

'You idiot!'

Unaware of my pleading, Tariq carried on with what he was doing with the same surgical precision he used to slice open the chests of his patients.

'You damned fool!' I cried. In silence, I watched as he went about dismembering my body. I watched and tried to make sense of the plan he had hatched to get out of this mess. First, he severed my arms and my legs from my torso. Then he bundled my upper limbs separately from my lower limbs before tying them with the same ropes I had used on him earlier. He searched for large trash bags and found some in the kitchen. After draining the blood out of my dismembered parts, he wiped them down and dried them before stashing them inside trash bags. He finished by mopping the room, giving the tiles a good scrub, and finally sterilizing the floor with Dettol.

'You're such a coward,' I berated him when he was done. 'Are you proud yourself? Has your fear blinded you to this degree?'

But I stopped when I saw him collapse on the floor next to the trash bag containing my body parts. He might have collapsed out of exhaustion or fear. Or it might have been grief or remorse which finally made him crumble down and fall on his knees next to my body, sobbing.

'You're crying too? A big man like you crying?'

I was about to continue scolding him, but his agony and his tears transformed the anger consuming me to a feeling of guilt and responsibility. Wasn't I the one who betrayed him, leaving him in this unenviable situation? What else was he supposed to do? Leave my corpse where it was and flee the scene? Or pick his cell phone, call the police, and try to explain to them what happened, hoping against hope that they would believe him, only to bear the brunt of the scandal and the ensuing social consequences? Or should he have acted like an idiot and attempted to hide the body and flee as though nothing had happened?

Tariq was a smart man, but he chose to act stupidly. His actions confused me. I had no idea how to help him clamber out of the mess I had caused. Had he lost the ability to make sound decisions after I made him used to relying on me in every aspect of his life?

'Come on. Get up now. That's enough. This is not the time to cry,' I commanded him, trying to take control of the situation. This time, I felt him responding to me, as though what happened hadn't changed the nature of our relationship or affected my ability to control him as I wish. I watched him stand up and pick up the black garbage bags and head to the front door to leave, so I shouted, 'No! Not that way. Use the back door!'

It seemed that he heard me. He stopped a few feet away from the main door, turned around and left through the back door.

CHAPTER 2

IS THIS HOW YOU LIKE IT, HONEY?

FIRAS

I AM fairly sure that my disappearance from the face of earth has been a constant wish nurtured by my husband Firas for months, ever since he realized that our married life had left him unable to mold me into the image of his choice. Like other men, he saw himself in control of any relationship he had with women. And like them, he tried to exploit any and all inherited social privileges left at the disposal of his gender to control me. What he failed to realize was that I, like many other women, never fell for those lies society tried to impose on us.

Firas's imagination must have crafted various scenarios for my death, perhaps as the result of a car crash caused by my reckless driving. But unlike the vague idea of death occasionally crossing my mind, Firas's fantasy was a wish he could hardly wait to see fulfilled.

'If you'd only died, it would have been better for the two of us!' That was my husband's response yesterday when I told him I had narrowly avoided a collision with a speeding car near Um Uthaina intersection. I felt punched in the stomach when I heard his words, even though his aggressive attitude no longer fazed me. I was used to his peculiarities by then, having been married to him for two years preceded by the full year I spent trying to know him better. During those three years, I realized that he wasn't capable of forgiving anyone who offended him. On the contrary, he was weak and vulnerable. He felt slighted by everything, even things which did not amount to insults, and he was quick to offend others if he felt his dignity was threatened.

I should have expected that response from him after the way I rejected him the same morning when he rubbed against me and wanted to have sex. Nevertheless, I was surprised at his audacity in voicing his wish to see me dead, just like that.

He was rude when he crept up to me in the bathroom as I was brushing my teeth. He hugged me from behind, and, making sure I felt the bulge in his pants, he swept my hair from my shoulder, his lips ready to plant a kiss on my neck. He still wanted to impose his manhood on me as if his limited way of thinking could not accept the fact that I was repulsed by him. As if his ears were tuned deaf every time I said in no uncertain terms, 'If I've told you once, I've told you a thousand times: I don't want you!'

My entire body trembled the second I felt him close to me. My muscles tensed and my blood boiled. I tried to control myself and avoid any kind of overblown reaction, but he was shameless. He didn't care. He was enjoying the burst of male hormones gushing through his veins, ready to act on the urge coursing through his body. I let him plant his kiss on me as I resisted an overwhelming desire to grab the perfume bottle in front of me and spray it in his eyes or to bite his arm, right on the cut I inflected on him the day before. He would have screamed in pain as he hurled a torrent of insults at me, or he would have probably slapped me or lunged at me, trying to hit and hurt me worse than I had hurt him. I would have responded in kind, slapping him back if he slapped me, clawing his face with my nails, or kicking him in the balls to teach him never to do that to me again.

But I was wise and acted fast. I ignored his erection pressed up against me. I finished brushing my teeth and put the toothbrush down. I took a sip of water, rinsed my mouth, spat the water out, and then quickly turned off the tap and quietly peeled myself away, leaving the bathroom as if nothing had happened. He followed me a minute later, a wicked smile on his face.

I realized that his mind refused to register that I was rejecting him, so he decided to think of my reaction as part of a game. A chase where he was the predator and I the prey. The idea of him as the predator gave him a sense of power, while my resistance translated in his mind as a chance to prove his dominance over me, an invitation to reassert his masculinity. He must have viewed it as fake resistance, the kind prevalent in Egyptian movies. A form of coquettish hard-to-get play used by women to entice men and turn them on. At the end of such a scenario, in his mind, after a few flirtatious moves and acts of fake modesty, I was bound to fall into his arms, surrender to his masculinity, capitulate to his virility.

I was a predator. I didn't think much of the chase unless I was the one doing the chasing, the one breaking a man, reducing him to a meek lamb. Obedient, submissive. Under my control. I had to act firmly when Firas stealthily slunk up behind me as I stood in front of the mirror clasping my bra. I spun around and looked him straight in the eye. 'What do you want?'

'Gosh! You're so stubborn,' he huffed, as if he didn't expect my question, or was too embarrassed to come out and just say he wanted me.

'I'm the one who's stubborn?' I snapped, turning my back to him. I picked up my eyeliner and leaned forward, closer to the mirror.

'Yes. You. You're so stubborn!' He yelled at me.

'And so are you!' I yelled back as I opened my eye wide to line it with kohl.

"Oh, come on. Let's give it a try,' he said suddenly,

changing his tone, trying to win me over.

'We've tried plenty of times, Firas. You want something and I want something else,' I replied, unmoved.

'See how stubborn you are? You insist on acting like the man in bed.'

I stopped doing my eyeliner and fixed a sharp gaze on him. 'Fuck off!' I said, before adding cynically, 'Shouldn't you first know what being a man really means?'

'Respect yourself and act like a lady!' he yelled.

'Act like a lady?' I almost fell to the floor laughing. 'Yes, sir. Whatever you say, honey. If you say so, darling. I'll respect my self and act like a lady, just like you want me to.' I smoothed my long hair behind my ears and spun around to face him. I put my finger in my mouth, licking it and tilting my head as I gazed at him seductively, adopting the flirtatious Syrian accent of the women from *Bab al-Hara1*. 'Is this how you like it, babe? What can I do for you, my king, my universe?'

Dumbfounded, he watched me carry on with my playacting, making fun of him.

'I'm at your beck and call, love,' I teased. I took two steps toward the bed and sat down gently, pouting like Haifa Wehbe in her "Boos El Wawa" music video. I pressed my knees together, lay my head on the pillow, and, running my fingers across my breasts, whispered seductively, 'Come on then. Come and get it.'

But before he could make a move, I flicked the switch, changing my tone of voice and my body language.

'I know it's how you want me to be,' I said, standing up and adopting a serious tone. I raised my head to look him in the eye and added, 'But I'm not like that and I will never be like that. Not for you and not for anyone else. Got it?'

---

1   *Bab al-Hara* is a Syrian drama series set in the 1920s. The first
    series (season), directed by Bassam al-Mulla, was aired in 2006.

I said that and went back to what I was doing, ignoring him. As I finished getting dressed, I could see him in the mirror, perplexed, astonished, his eyes fixed on me.

'I'm the idiot who married a nutcase!' He yelled after a few seconds had passed, right before storming out of the room and slamming the door behind him.

I took a deep breath after he left. I stood in front of the mirror examining my facial expression. I couldn't help thinking: was I right to treat him like that? Did he deserve it?

I finished fixing my hair, picked up my purse and left the room. I looked for him and found him in the kitchen pouring himself a glass of milk and eating a sandwich. He pretended I wasn't there. I stood silently. I couldn't bring myself to apologize to him. And knowing him, I didn't expect him to apologize, either.

I left him like that and went out. A couple of hours later, I called to smooth things over between us. His tone on the phone suggested he had forgotten what happened. So, when I described to him the details of the near-miss car accident, I was actually attempting to diffuse the tension between us and get things back to normal. That's why expressing his wish for my death was particularly vile and uncalled-for.

The next day, unprompted, I fulfilled his fantasy, leaving him wallowing in remorse, wishing he could turn back the clock to forty-eight hours before, to stop himself from forming the very thought he had dared utter out loud.

CHAPTER 3

THE MOST REALISTIC SCENARIO

FIRAS

IF fate had only loved Firas the way his mother loved him, it would have delayed my death for a few hours until he returned from his hunting trip. I had intended to confront him with my final decision to leave him. Or fate could have made him return earlier to find me in bed with another man. He would have lost his mind. Blinded by rage, he would likely have acted in a manner widely viewed in Jordan to be within his rights: killed me to rid himself of me.

According to the traditional scenario, Firas walks into the house quietly. In his right hand, he is carrying the birds he has shot, the hunting rifle slung over his left shoulder. He is just about to lay the birds down on the kitchen table when he hears a man's voice coming from the bedroom. The first thought that crosses his mind is that a thief has broken into the house, but the man's screams confuse him. Firas hesitates. He might consider running out of the house and calling the police, but then he hears my voice. Cautiously, he approaches the room to hear better. His blood starts boiling even before he knows for certain what's happening behind the door, before he sees it with his own eyes. He bursts into the room, confident that society and the law are on his side. His suspicions are confirmed. He finds me naked in bed with another man. I tremble with fear and grab the bed sheets to cover my body. I scream when I see him raise the rifle and aim it at my chest. I beg him to forgive me. I beseech him not to shoot me. He doesn't hear me. Blinded by rage, he pulls the trigger.

My name appears on the latest list of honor-killing victims. The next day, it is published in the official newspaper. I might be the fifteenth or twentieth victim this year. What's the difference? The story will not refer to me as a virgin. Readers might view me as an adulteress rather than a victim. The public might rally in defense of Firas. There will be a call for him to be released, his sentence commuted. After all, he is the victim of betrayal. My infidelity has pushed him to kill me. He will become a national hero, the epitome of the true Middle Eastern male: a man who does not stand by silently when a stain tarnishes his honor, a man who dutifully does all it takes to protect his name.

Perhaps the most realistic scenario is what would have happened if fate had brought him home earlier. Fate would have had him walk into the house quietly, carrying the birds he had shot. The rest of the story would follow the same traditional narrative as above, up until the point he hears a man's voice coming from the bedroom. But he wouldn't think it was a thief and wouldn't walk toward the room to confirm what he had just heard. He would hesitate a bit, thinking quickly of the right course of action. Should he burst in on me and my lover? Discovering the shameful sight, would he scream hysterically and throw himself on the other man, fight him to death? He might overcome the other man and kill him, or the other man might get the better of him and kill *him*. In a situation like that, and with the enormity of social pressure surrounding it, he would end up either murdering the other man or killed by him. In the first scenario, he would redeem his honor and somehow restore his reputation which would be tarnished once it became known that his virility was not enough for his wife, who had cheated on him with another man. In the second scenario, he would lose his life after losing his dignity. He might prefer the second option, having been brought up in a society that associates masculinity with washing away shame and disgrace with blood. He is fully aware that society can inflict the harshest pain on him if he commits just one mistake or does anything to indicate he is cowardly or weak.

However, Firas, unlike Tariq, is quick-thinking in difficult situations. In fact, had he come in and caught us in the act, I doubt that he would have done anything reckless or put himself in an embarrassing position. He would have slipped out quietly and left the house, only to return later and confront me when I was alone. He would treat me with contempt and detest me for the rest of his life, eventually divorcing me and doing everything he could to tear my reputation to shreds.

But, of course, fate didn't smile down on Firas, so this is what actually happened. My soul, having just left my body, floated off and hovered in a strange, ethereal space. I don't know how much time had passed. I suddenly saw myself sitting in the passenger seat in Firas's car, next to him. We were stuck in traffic on Medical City Street due to an accident, just like the one he had wished for me. The gridlocked traffic caused him to come home late. I found myself sympathizing with him, sensing his thoughts in a way I never did before. I could see him walking among the trees in the Ajlun Mountains, searching for birds to shoot. He seemed distracted, unable to concentrate, struggling to aim and hit his target. Moments later, I saw him stretched out on a large rock in the woods amidst cypress and pine trees, his thoughts drifting with his eyes across the sky.

Unlike Newton, who sat under an apple tree contemplating nature, Firas's dilemma did not revolve around the nature of the universe. There was no need for an apple to fall on his head to solve it. He was woken from his reverie when the dropping of a bird, one of those wretched little nightingales he was trying to shoot, fell on his forehead. For Firas, it was a moment of awakening. Startled, he jumped up and angrily wiped his forehead, cursing his rotten luck. But then, as he sat down, calmer, a thought occurred to him. Gravity, the attraction of cosmic bodies to each other, was no different from sexual attraction. Physiology had much in common with physics, he thought, sharing its fundamental laws, and most importantly, the law of gravity. In physiology, as with physics, like poles repel and opposite poles attract.

Right then, Firas came to the same conclusion I had come to, and he hurried back home to divorce me. As fate willed it, he was meant to cross paths with Tariq at the 8th Circle junction, each in his own black Peugeot of the same model. They were two men brought together by the same car, the same woman, the same building. They hardly knew each other, nothing to warrant more than a passing hello. And now they were in the grip of this notorious junction with its usual midday traffic. Firas was heading in the direction of the 7th Circle, determined to put an end to this phase of his life, while Tariq, distracted, lost, was driving in the opposite direction.

Seeing Tariq, I felt my soul shift from the passenger seat next to Firas to settle close to Tariq in the other Peugeot. As with Firas moments ago, I began to read Tariq's thoughts and feel his pain. His thoughts revolved around what do with my body. He had hurled the bag into the trunk of his car before setting off in a hurry, but instead of coming out from behind Cozmo and heading straight onto Airport Road, he found himself in the wrong lane on Safeway Bridge. Crossing the bridge toward Sweifieh, he exited at the 6th Circle and drove back toward the airport, making sure to take the 7th Circle tunnel to avoid getting delayed by its traffic light. He managed to avoid the traffic lights, but instead found himself in the middle of a traffic jam at the 8th Circle, waiting for the traffic cop to wave him through. Seeing the policewoman terrified him. He thought that his crime, a crime which he had not even committed, had been discovered. He expected the cop to stop him at any moment. And if that happened, he had no idea what to do. He would most likely panic and try to flee again. I felt his hands tremble on the steering wheel even though there were times when he was turned on by fantasizing about being arrested, imprisoned, and tortured by a policewoman. I saw him struggle to keep his fingers away from the horn when it seemed to him that what he had long fantasized about was about to become a reality. His heart almost stopped when he mistook the cop's hand gesture to stop the cars in his lane as a signal for him specifically to stop. He looked in the rearview mirror to make sure the trunk was locked and hadn't burst open. He tried to stop himself from visualizing blood oozing out my corpse, seeping out from the trunk and dripping on the ground in plain view, despite all the precautions he had taken.

Just when he thought it couldn't get worse, he saw Firas's car enter the roundabout. The fact that it was the same color and model caught his eye, but he was quick to look away the moment he spotted Firas at the wheel. Firas didn't see him. He was distracted, busy musing over what people would think of him after his divorce. He pulled out in front of Tariq heading home, as Tariq turned off in the direction of the airport.

In a flash, I left Tariq and was spirited away home, watching Firas enter, carrying his three birds, his only kill from the morning's hunting trip. He dropped the birds in the kitchen sink, hung up his rifle, and headed to the bedroom to change his clothes. After establishing I wasn't home, he went to the living room and switched the TV on. He let a quarter of an hour pass before calling me. My phone rang in Tariq's car. My spirit flitted back to Tariq, who jumped in his seat, startled by the ringtone.

Tariq quickly fumbled for the phone and read the caller's name. He didn't answer and didn't end the call. Instead, he waited for the phone to stop ringing. He pulled over to the side of the road and entered my passcode. To avoid raising any suspicions, he didn't delete all data from the phone but searched for our WhatsApp chats and deleted them. He browsed the photo albums for anything pertaining to him and deleted those photos too. He looked up his number in my contacts and deleted it. He made sure his number no longer showed up in the "Recents" list. He opened my Facebook app, searched for my "Empress of All Men" private page, and deleted it. After that, he switched off the phone, opened up the back, and removed the SIM card so the police wouldn't be able to track it.

Tariq couldn't think clearly about what to do with my body. It was still the middle of the day and driving on Airport Road meant the risk of getting stopped by one of the many police patrols. At the same time, if he chose to get off the main road and head to a remote unfamiliar area, he would risk being questioned by the locals or followed by the local police. His options were limited, each worse than the other, and his nerves could hardly take the stress. He wanted to get rid of my body fast, regardless of how he did it, so he drove around looking out for a dumpster, cursing the local authorities for not providing more of them. He finally spotted one on the service road parallel to Airport Road. Quickly, he slammed on the brakes, grabbed the bag containing my body out of the trunk, and hurled it into the dumpster. He made a point of not turning his head or looking around to see if anyone had seen him, trying to make his movements look normal to avoid attracting attention, which he successfully managed to do.

In the stress of the moment, he forgot to throw my cell phone in with my body. He only remembered when he turned into our street. This time, he looked out for a trash can closer than the dumpster on the street corner to throw the phone in it, but he couldn't find one. Instead, he spotted Firas's car, and for the first time since that morning, he made a calculated move. I was taken back when Tariq got out of the car and walked quietly over to Firas's car. Strolling casually and barely stopping, he reached down and dropped my cell phone on the ground under the car.

I never realized before that moment that Tariq was capable of such astute thinking, and I wasn't sure at that point if his intention was to incriminate Firas or not. To put the phone in a spot familiar to me may have been the easiest way to get rid of it. But, with that swift action, he saved himself from the noose and instead, wrapped the rope around Firas's neck.

CHAPTER 4

A MAN IS LIKE A COIL SPRING UNDER YOUR FOOT

FIRAS & TARIQ

FIRAS was unaware of what had recently taken place around him. The house seemed clean and tidy, exactly as he left in the morning. There was no indication of the dreadful events which unfolded within its walls a short while ago. The front door and the kitchen door were locked, my house keys already in the dumpster on Airport Road, along with my body. The bedroom was as he usually found it when he came back from his hunting trips on Saturdays: a bright white bedspread had replaced the one Tariq shoved in the washing machine. The waxed floor gleaming and clean. The curtains drawn shut.

Firas watched television for some time. When he got bored and felt sleepy, he lay down on the bed to take a short nap. Two floors above, Tariq had just arrived home. Neither his wife nor any of his kids were there. He felt exhausted and climbed into bed. As for me, I was occupying the ethereal space between them, hovering around, accompanying each one separately and both at the same time. I found I was able to dip into their memories and blend them with my own, to sense their feelings and remain aware of mine at the same time. Memories flashed across my eyes. I was adrift in an eddy of past events, caught in the film reel of the drama of my life. Firas's thoughts drifted all the way to our wedding night, while Tariq replayed the memories of our first chat on Facebook in his mind.

In Firas's mind, I appeared in angelic delicate form,

wearing my silk wedding dress, its whiteness adding a touch of innocence to my face. I drifted gracefully across the dance floor in his arms, letting him lead me, turning me left and right to the beat of romantic music. A demure bride as was expected of me. An obedient wife as dictated by tradition.

In Tariq's memory, the words of my first message on our private chat were an arrow aimed straight at his heart. The message I sent him was short and to the point. My words drew him in, stirring inside him feelings and desires he had long dreamed of experiencing. We first met on a private Facebook page I had created a year before. That page was my own space, a playground for my imagination. There, I created a parallel life, constructed my own fantasies, lived in a dream world.

I set it up just like some other profile pages I had come across on Facebook, hidden from plain view. Pages by women like me who were into BDSM and were turned on by the control and power they wielded upon submissive men. But on the privacy settings, I made my page public, open for anyone to visit. I disclosed my sexual preferences but kept everything else about me private. A few days after I set up the page, Tariq stumbled across it. The page might have been new, but it caught his eye as well as the eyes of the hordes of other men who soon flocked to it, eager to bow at my feet. It could have been the title that lured them, or the scintillating steamy photos I found online and shared on my page. I posted regular updates with pictures of overbearing leather-clad women towering over naked men who cowered at their feet. Or it might have been the posts I wrote that turned men who viewed my page on and kept them coming in droves. On the day Tariq found the page, I had posted:

> *"A man is like a coil spring under your foot. Don't remove the pressure or he'll bounce back and slap you on the cheek."*

His comment on my post was brief and in keeping with the sexual personality he wanted to project at the time: *"Quite right, Ma'am. We're your slaves. We prostrate ourselves at your feet."*

I had made a decision not to respond to any comments as a way of preserving the sense of superiority I had created with the photos I posted of dominant women, but I would occasionally click on the profile photos of men who visited my page. It was obvious that like me, they used fake identities for these erotic chats.

When I visited Tariq's page, I discovered that he was as cautious as the others. There were no photos of him except for a blurry photo from which it was hard to make out his features. Along with that, I found a few comments he had left on the pages of other dominatrices, suggesting the same meekness and servility he showed toward me.

I liked the look of him. His photo might have been overexposed, but from what I could see, he looked like the kind of men I tended to go for, traditional masculine look and all. I could tell he was middle-aged with thinning hair, pale skin, a stubbly chin and a thick moustache. His build suggested physical strength without being excessively muscular.

Had I bumped into him on the street, I might have found him intimidating. But I met him on Facebook, on my page. On my terms. From my experience with guys like him, I knew exactly how he thought. So, without knowing any specifics about his life, I felt bold enough to send him a direct message saying, *"As of today, consider yourself my property."*

Tariq's eyes lit up as he remembered the moment when I claimed possession over him, just as Firas's imagination flashed up with a memory of the moment he thought he owned me.

On our wedding night, at the Sheraton on Fifth Circle, Firas carried me through the door into our bridal suite. He wanted to start our married life with this familiar gesture that he had seen on TV and in films, where the groom carries his bride over the threshold on their wedding night. At the time, I interpreted his move as romantic. This was a man's unspoken declaration of physical and psychological readiness to do anything for the comfort of his bride. But I later came to see it as the first move a husband would take to assert his power, control, and guardianship over his wife. No longer able to stand on her own two feet, the bride would enter her new life clinging to her husband's neck, allowing him to steer her future in the direction of his choosing.

Despite his exhaustion after a long day of festivities, despite the weight of my bulky wedding dress, and despite me telling him not to carry me, fearing he was going to drop me before he reached the bed, Firas stuck to his plan, half carrying, half dragging me. Swaying right and left as he staggered into the room, he quickened his steps before dropping me on to the nearest sofa. He stood close to me laughing, trying to catch his breath before joking, 'Phew! What did you have for dinner tonight?'

His joke could have quite easily killed the mood, but I was in love with him back then, so I clung to the romantic appeal of the moment.

That was my wedding night with Firas. If I were to reconstruct the night all again, but with Tariq this time lifting me over the threshold, I would have willingly let him do it. I wouldn't look at it as an expression of male power or view it as a romantic gesture. I would do it my way. I would stand up tall and straight, look down on him, and command him to carry me into the room. I would order him to tense his muscles, hold me firmly, and walk slowly and steadily to the sofa and lay me down gently. Seat his queen on her throne.

But that night I wasn't a queen. I was an ordinary bride.

The queen inside me was tethered by the ropes of modesty, fettered by the shackles of social expectations, restrained by the handcuffs of sexual inexperience and naïveté. No one had told me about the importance of sexual harmony in marital relations or explained to me that there was a side to it a woman might not enjoy. My husband placed total trust in the masculine role he had inherited. He seemed happy with the role he was supposed to assume in marriage, even before our life as a couple had started. He expected everything to be done according to custom and tradition.

I was shy that night, too meek to express my desire openly. Or perhaps I didn't fully understand that desire in me as I know it today. I didn't need to be shy with Firas because I had known him a year prior to our marriage. We had fumbled and explored each other's bodies, even if we didn't go all the way. I remember him criticizing me back then, remarking on how intensely I kissed him and how the way I made out with him as being "crass" or 'like a guy". He assumed that he was meant to take the initiative. My attempts to influence things in the bedroom didn't fit with his idea of how a woman should behave. Firas's criticism saddened and disappointed me. In response, I tried to restrain myself and curb my libido. I let him snuff my desire as he held me and kissed me the way he wanted.

In another version of our wedding night – the way I remember it – I surprised him by standing on the sofa where he had just seated me. I turned and gave him a gentle shove so he fell on the sofa where I was sitting a few minutes before, then I jumped down and sat on his lap. I grabbed his arms and raised them over his head. He laughed in surprise.

He didn't resist me at first. I pressed down on his arms to stop him from moving and he remained still as I covered him with hungry kisses. He soon began to resist, agitated by the situation he found himself in. He tried to shake off my grip, but he was exhausted and I was the one in the stronger position. He struggled to push me off but I applied more pressure to hold him down, forcing him to surrender to me. He jerked his arms away violently and I became self-conscious. The expression on his face changed. He seemed serious. He wanted me to take it easy.

'What's wrong?' I asked, unhappy with his reaction. But he didn't answer.

I didn't want the night to take a wrong turn, so I rested my head on his chest apologetically. I let him put his arms around me and he became gentle and tender once again. I let him take the lead as we resumed our foreplay. I succumbed to his hands as he caressed and kissed me with the level of tenderness expected on a wedding night. Once the mood was reestablished, I stood up and asked him to help me out of my wedding dress and went to the bathroom to take a hot bath. I came back to the room the bride Firas had expected. With a bit of romance, we carried on where we had left off.

The fact that we remembered it so differently suggests that we must have realized back then that our sexual desires were incompatible. We tried to ignore our differences in the months that followed, but each sexual encounter between us sounded an alarm bell, warning us that we were ultimately unsuited for each other.

CHAPTER 5

THAT SUMBISSIVE LOOK IN HIS EYES!

TARIQ

WHEN I announced to Tariq that he was now my "property", it was done in the virtual world. And when he immediately acquiesced to me, even if it was informally and just in words, neither one of us knew exactly how this relationship of dominance and control would develop, inflaming our carnal desires with such force until it eventually broke free and spilled into our real world.

Facebook gave us the privacy we craved in the beginning. Initially, we felt no pressure to reveal our true identities. What started between us was mere words. Until then, neither one of us had seen the other's face, body, or even a complete photo. Words were enough. And because it was a relationship of words alone, it conveyed a certain truth. Our conversations carried with them the deep desires we were both afraid to declare to our spouses. The screen we hid behind freed our words from the demands of modesty. And since my desire to impose control over him was matched by his desire to submit to me, the power disparity between us grew. So too did our sexual desire. We stayed up late and spent hours chatting on our phones.

'How are you today, Ma'am?'

'Good.'

'How can I serve you?'

'Kneel down to your mistress.'

'I am kneeling down before you.'

'I'm the Queen and you're my slave.'

'At your service. I'm here to serve your beauty.'

'When I speak to you, bow your head down. Understood?'

'Yes, Ma'am. My head is always bowed to the ground at your feet.'

Soon enough, Tariq got used to bowing his head to me in deference to please me. I remember that in those first chats on Messenger, I avoided referring explicitly to our genitalia. I think I was still too shy, a byproduct of the way I was brought up. But I didn't hold back from speaking down to him and I didn't know why it gave me such a buzz. Later, I discovered that the way I addressed him turned him on as much as it did me. He was strongly drawn to me and by treating him in an overbearing manner, I made him want me even more.

I traced that need back to a desire within me to shatter what I couldn't control in my daily life. I was afraid of men as a child. As I grew up, I was aware of a male culture that amplified masculinity and presented men as superior to women and therefore had the right to control of them. My relationship with Tariq gave me the chance to tear up that ingrained image and defy the prevailing social roles and assumptions I had imbibed in my childhood. The result was exhilarating.

At that time, I didn't understand why he was so keen to submit to me or why being humiliated and belittled turned him on. I couldn't explain his attachment to me or his eagerness to make me happy and serve my every need. Society, as I saw it, placed value on power, control, and pride, instilling those feelings in men and women alike. Personally, I interpreted the strength of my desires partly as a need to emphasize and reinforce the value of my own sexuality, a need to hold on to my femininity and celebrate it in a way that made sense and felt right to me. But I couldn't help wondering why a mature strong man, a professional with high social standing like Tariq, would find pleasure in being humiliated and demeaned like that.

I asked him about it once when we met in private, after my feelings for him became strong, and I was desperate to understand what was going on in his mind. That day, I ordered him in advance to have tub of hot water ready to wash my feet when I got to the hotel room. He was to appear barefoot in his pajamas and to bow down to me when I entered the room.

And indeed, as soon I walked into the room, Tariq welcomed me with his head bowed down. He took my bag from my hand and put it on the side table and helped me take off my coat. He headed over to the closet to hang it up, exactly as I had trained him.

I missed him and desperately wanted him, especially then in his white flannel pajama top, as he showed perfectly complete deference to me. I strode over to the closet to check if he had hung my coat up properly, then I stuck my finger between his shoulders and shoved him against the closet. He was big and it wasn't easy to push him, especially given the fact that he was a few centimeters taller than me, but my high heels gave me more of a height advantage than usual. He was barefoot which made me slightly taller than him. I liked that. I grabbed his shoulder to and spun him around to face me. He obediently followed my lead. I stepped closer and pressed my chest against his as I stared firmly into his eyes.

Oh, how I loved that submissive look in his eyes!

I knew my proximity to him drove him wild, but I had taught him to stand still and not to dare think about touching my breast or any part of my body until I allowed him to do so. Without uttering a sound, and as I continued to stare at him, he placed his hands behind his back. He bent his head forward and remained in that position, motionless. I grabbed his neck and pulled him forward to kiss him on the lips before turning my back and walking away. I wanted to catch my breath and let our desire rage longer. I strutted proudly over toward the sofa and waited for him to follow me.

'Did you add salt to the water?' I asked, pointing at tub.

'Yes, Ma'am. Just as you ordered,' he answered, his voice rough and humble, before crouching down to pull my shoes off my feet. He placed them on the floor side by side and rushed to the bathroom for a towel.

I was exhausted after a long day at work and my feet were aching in my tight shoes. I was looking forward to his wonderful invigorating foot massage.

'Relax, Ma'am,' he said, picking up a cushion and clearing the sofa so I could sit down comfortably. He sat cross-legged on the floor in front of me and ran his fingers through the water to make sure the temperature was right before lifting my feet and placing them in the tub.

'Ma'am, I brought you a gift from Paris as promised.' He clearly couldn't wait to show me. He jumped up to fetch the gift from the side table and handed it to me before resuming his previous position in front of me. He lifted my left foot out of the water and gently patted it dry with the towel, then he breathed in the clean scent of my toes, kissed them, and tenderly placed my foot on the floor.

There were two gifts in fact. The first one, long and thin like a golf club, was carefully wrapped in wrapping paper. The second one small, in a rectangular box, like the packaging for a cell phone.

'Open the small one,' Tariq urged me eagerly.

I opened it up and found a cotton eye mask, similar to the masks passengers wear to sleep on airplanes. I smiled and put it to one side. 'And what's this one?' I asked.

'Open it and find out for yourself,' he answered, as he put pressure on the sole of my foot.

Slowly, I peeled off the wrapping paper to reveal a long cane with leather strips at one end. I held it from the other end and raised it to his face. I knew immediately what it was for, but still I asked him, 'What is this?'

'A whip, Ma'am.'

'Ah! So now I can teach you manners?' I said as I tightened my grip on the whip and brought it down lightly on his shoulder.

I laughed when he trembled. The third time I struck him, he recoiled way from me and put his hand on his shoulder.

'Does it hurt?' I asked, still laughing.

'It stings, Ma'am.'

'Good,' I replied. 'Come closer.'

I stood up in front of him and picked up the eye mask. I gestured to him to look down before placing the mask neatly over his eyes and pushing him back.

'Keep your hands behind your back.'

I cracked the whip and snapped it, hitting him on different parts of his body. I focused my blows mainly on his buttocks without inflicting too much, careful not to leave any marks or welts his wife might notice.

Whenever a blow came, Tariq moved his hand involuntarily to touch the place the whip had struck. I varied my strokes and moved from one side to the other faster than he could move his hand. I sped up and reduced the intensity of my movement based on his response.

'I told you. Keep your hands behind your back. Don't move!'

'Sorry, Ma'am.'

'Move them again and I'll tie them up.'

I carried on whipping him until he could take the blows without moving his hands. Then I moved closer to him and uncovered his eyes. As I sat back down, I grabbed his head and pulled him to me. I felt his body trembling. I looked in his eyes. He was struggling to hold back tears.

He remained quiet in spite of the pain I had inflicted on him. I ran my fingers affectionately through his hair and kissed his forehead. Leaning closer, I whispered in his ear: 'I love you.' I lifted his chin to savor the taste of his lips. I let him rest a moment on my chest before I ordered him to carry me to the bed. He jumped to his feet and lifted me gently and walked steadily with me in his arms, bending forward to lower me softly onto the bed. I asked him to get in bed with me, and I found my way into his arms, nestling my head on his shoulder. I put my hand on his chest, then tickled my fingers over his nipples, feeling them harden. When I felt him get hard, I slid my fingers down his abdomen to feel for his erection. Gripping his hard dick, I whispered playfully into his ear, 'Do you know why you're circumcised?'

'It's *sunnah*, Ma'am,' he answered, as if the answer were self-evident.

'I know it's the *sunnah*, love. But where does the custom come from?' I enjoyed testing him, always ready to show off my vast knowledge, especially on topics most people didn't know much about.

'It was God's commandment to Abraham and his descendants,' Tariq said with confidence.

'Yeah, that's the theological story. But did you know that circumcision was practiced before the emergence of the Abrahamic religions?'

'Really?' he exclaimed, surprised. He waited for me to explain.

'Yup, really. I read about it in Youssef Ziedan's novel *The Shadow of the Serpent*,'[2] I added to lend credibility to my claim. 'It's a wonderful book where Ziedan shows the decline in the significance of women historically. According to Ziedan, in the past, at the time when believed in female deity, a man would remove his foreskin and present it to the goddess to permit him to marry. With that gesture, he became clean and was permitted to sleep with women.'

I moved my fingers to stroke the tip of his penis. 'And you are clean and pure, honey. Which means you are permitted to sleep with me,' I said, winking at him. He smiled in agreement and was about to say something, but I stopped him. 'Wait. I'm not done.'

I put my finger on his lips and carried on with my story. 'In the novel, Ziedan says that a man who chose to become a monk would tie a string around balls until his balls shriveled and fell off. He would then place them on the doorstep of a rich man in his village. The rich man would then become responsible for the monk and provide him with the sustenance he needed to dedicate his time and life to serving the female deity.' I smiled cunningly and asked him, 'What do you think?'

'About what?' he answered, not getting my point.

'You offer me your manhood.' I clasped his balls. 'We tie your balls until they dry up and fall off so you can dedicate yourself and life to serving me.'

He laughed. 'You're nuts, Ma'am.'

I squeezed his balls until he moaned. 'And so are you.'

---

2   *The Shadow of the Serpent* is a novel by Egyptian author and ancient manuscript scholar Youssef Ziedan about the historical significance of women and their demotion culturally from a former position of sanctity and deification to one of desecration and denigration by men. It was published in 2006 by Dar al-Shorouk in Cairo.

I snuggled up against him, still holding his balls, kissed him on the lips, and added, 'And that's why you love me.'

I let go of his balls, lifted my head from his chest and hugged his head to mine. I wanted to hug him instead of letting him hug me. I ran my fingers in his hair tenderly as I thought of our relationship and how it did not conform to the expected norms of sexual relations between men and women. How could our desires and sexual preferences be at odds with all that's socially accepted and known? And why did our culture encourage women to be submissive to men, sexually and otherwise, ignoring the existence of men who sought the opposite? The strange thing was that no one mentioned those men or talked about them, as if dominance was a trait synonymous with manhood and virility while submissiveness was peculiar to women.

'I'm crazy about you, Ma'am. I love you.' Tariq's voice snatched me away from the train of my thoughts, but the questions themselves never left me.

I asked him jokingly, 'So in the eyes of others, am I the man and you're the woman, Tariq?'

He laughed. 'What do they know? There is nothing better than a strong woman. For me, femininity is power, attitude, resolute and absolute might.'

I liked what he said, so I asked him, 'And what about masculinity?'

'Masculinity is achieved by serving women.' His answer grounded me. I wanted to provoke him, so I asked him, 'This means you're a fulfilled man? A real man?'

'Yes, Ma'am. By the full definition of the word. In fact, my manhood is meaningless without serving you.'

I was hesitant to ask him, but I mustered enough courage to do so. 'Why are you turned on by serving me, Tariq?'

'I don't know. I've always been weak in the presence of strong women. Their beauty and power rob me of my strength, and that weakness turns me on.' He was quiet for a second, thinking, before he kissed my hand and added, 'Or maybe it's because in my everyday life, I'm the one in charge of everything. My house. My kids. The hospital. My family. I'm always the decision-maker, the one who has the final word. It's different with you. When I'm with you, I forget everything. I leave it all to you.' He was quiet again. 'When I see a woman this strong and full of self-confidence,' he added reflectively, 'I become a tame lion. A dog seeking her approval.'

'I love your submissiveness.'

'Are you happy with me, Ma'am?'

'Yes, I am. Now show me how you can please your mistress,' I commanded him.

He understood what I wanted right away. Raising his head from my chest, he burrowed under the covers, between my legs and licked me raw.

I was panting heavily. Holding his head, I asked for more until I felt my climax course through my body like an electric current. He smiled, happy that he could satisfy me. He put his head on my chest, content that he had fulfilled his duty. I hugged him and whispered in his ear, 'Thank you.'

CHAPTER 6

HIS ATTEMPTS TO CONTROL ME PROVOKED ME

FIRAS

I WATCHED Firas open his eyes, waking up from the nap he took after he came back from his hunting trip. He lay in bed without moving his head, looking straight at the yellow smiling-face charm attached to my car keys, then at my purse on the nightstand. The charm looked like the smiley emoji on Internet chats. It was part of a beautiful memory we had.

The first time I met Firas was on the first floor of Salute Beer Garden in Jabal Amman. He was alone and I was with my friend Rawan. I got dressed up that night for our date. I wore a silk blouse with wide stripes and summer colors, covering one shoulder and exposing another. I had on a pair of low-rise jeans exposing my lower back and a part of my belly, revealing the butterfly tattoo on my hip and my bronze suntanned complexion after spending the previous day at the Dead Sea. Firas was taken back by my looks as he stood up to shake my hand, introducing himself. He stepped to the side for me to walk and sit across from him. I knew exactly how to steer a conversation with a man bewitched by my beauty and eager to attract my attention to him at all cost. The situation called for a mixture of self-confidence and graceful conversational style, showing little interest, if any, in the other person, asking direct questions without going into personal details – all of which I had mastered to a tee.

'What do you do for a living?' I asked him.

'I'm a marketing director,' he replied with confidence and

pride in his success at what he did.

I didn't want to satisfy his ego by complimenting his job, so I followed my question with another: 'Nice. You hold a degree in marketing then?'

'Yeah.'

'From which university?'

'University of Jordan.'

'And where do you live?'

'In Al Rabia.'

Such sessions usually ended in me gathering all the information I needed about the guy sitting in front of me while I remained mysterious and retained my charm in his eyes. On that first date, I found out all I needed to know about Firas and let him chase me afterwards to know me better.

Firas seemed like the perfect groom project. I was already aware of the rules of the game. In my teenage years, boys from the nearby boys' school used to race to reach my school, eager for a smile or a look of recognition from me. My previous experiences with men made me realize right away that Firas, like most other men, wanted what he couldn't get and lost interest in what he had. That's why I didn't reply to his calls, pretending to be busy. Alternately, I would stop texting back in the middle of us exchanging texts, only to come back and add a brief comment after a few hours had passed. In the beginning of our relationship, I met him once every two weeks and only after he begged to see me. I hardly ever repaid his compliments with compliments. It was a good strategy which succeeded in igniting his feelings toward me. After our initial date, I disappeared for weeks, leaving him to dream about seeing me again, eager to hear my voice, feeling he was on cloud nine just by imagining me.

But after two years of marriage, my voice started to irritate Firas and the mere sight of me angered him. It seemed that the smiley-face charm provoked him. I watched him get up angrily, grab the charm with the car keys, and stride toward the main door. He came back holding his own keychain, sat down on the bed, and removed the charm from my keychain and added it to his. When he was done, he gripped his keychain tightly in his fist before throwing it down beside himself on the bed. He lay down and exhaled, relieved, as though that simple act had reinforced his decision to kick me out of his life.

That day, the charm caught my eye as soon as I sat down, but I only mentioned it when we got up to leave. He was standing next to me as I waited for the valet service to bring my car.

'That's a nice piece,' I said, smiling, as I pointed at it. He was holding his keychain, flipping the smiley face between his fingers.

I had hardly uttered the words before Firas removed the charm from his keychain and put in my palm. 'It's yours now,' he said, closing my fingers around it.

I didn't protest because I liked it the same way I liked him that day. That was why I carried it with me from that day on, a witness to the start of our love. That gift left me with a good first impression of Firas. He was generous and well mannered. But that rosy picture didn't last long. Subsequent days revealed to me that his good manners were inversely proportional to our intimate relationship. Like a chameleon, he changed as my defenses fell, his true colors resurfacing when he no longer needed my approval or when he was confident that I was by his side, clinging to him. For months before that, he was ready to do anything, chase me for days on end until I fell prey to his love, only to change afterwards and go back to his old nature. When he sensed my feelings toward him cool and understood the seriousness of my hints for a divorce, he resorted to a deceptive show of love to stop our relationship from unraveling, only to go back to his old nature when he despaired at the possibility of saving our marriage, or when his anger at me overpowered his fear of my leaving.

Firas became aware of the time. It was six in the evening and I wasn't home yet. Irritated, he picked up his cell phone and dialed my number, but my phone was turned off. He texted Rawan to ask her about me, then threw the phone to the side. He touched the scar on his arm, apparently remembering what transpired between us two days before.

That day, I was dressed up and ready to leave the house when he asked me, 'Where are you going?'

'None of your business,' I snapped, and turned my back to leave. His constant attempts to control me irritated me and I no longer cared about his feelings.

He banged his fist on the living room table and yelled, 'When I ask you a question, you answer! Do you understand?'

As I turned to face him, he picked up his cell phone and threw it at me, but the phone missed and hit the wall behind me. Shaken, I froze in place, in utter disbelief at his rudeness and use of force. I was so angry. I wasn't going to sweep things under the rug and let Firas derive any satisfaction from scaring me, so I looked around for something to throw. I gripped the metal frame holding our wedding photo and threw it at him. Its sharp edge grazed his right arm as he held it up to protect his face. He screamed and called me crazy.

I saw blood dripping from his arm, but I didn't feel the need to apologize. There wasn't a lot of blood anyway. I never wanted to resort to violence, but he deserved what happened to him. He had to learn his lesson and know that he could never repeat what he did. I left him like that and headed out, fully aware that I had aimed and hit him because I didn't

intend to miss, while he missed me intentionally because all
he wanted was to scare me.

Firas pressed his finger against the scar as he lay on the bed
before picking up his cell phone again and running his fingers
across the cracked screen. There was no answer from Rawan.
He tried calling me again without any success, so he called
her one more time and asked her about me. She had no idea
where I was. He called a friend of mine asking if he knew my
whereabouts, but even that friend had no clue, so Firas waited
a couple of hours before trying to call me again. And then,
after two more hours had passed, he tried calling me one last
time before deciding to call my mom.

My mom wasn't a fan of Firas and hadn't approved of him
the minute I introduced him to her and my dad.

When I took Firas to meet my parents, he sat at the dining
table, switching to the good-guy personality, trying hard to
ingratiate himself with my parents in a squeamishly fawning
way in order to win them over.

'Auntie, the stuffed zucchini is so delicious.'

'Uncle, you look in great health.'

'Auntie, the top you're wearing is stunning.'

'Uncle, I love the layout of the house.'

My mom put up with his compliments and hid her
disapproval of him. At the same time, she didn't try to convince
me to change my mind about marrying him because she
respected me and valued my choices. That was how she raised
me, independent and confident. She would have liked for me
to marry my cousin. She was convinced that he was better for
me, but she forced herself to accept Firas even though she
saw his shortcomings much better than I did. Every once in
a while, she would ask me about my feelings toward him to
make sure I loved him, reassuring me that marriage was not the

end of the world. Marriage might be a serious commitment, she told me, a commitment that could prove hard to break away from, but she would still stand by me and support me if I decided to change my mind about Firas, be it during our engagement or after our marriage. My mother told me that the most important thing in the world was my happiness, that nothing should ever make me give it up for a man.

My mother sounded irritated at Firas when he called to inform her that I wasn't home yet. I had told her that morning that he threw his cell phone at me.

'Is everything all right, Firas?' she asked him.

'Yes, Auntie. Do you know where Laila is?' he asked her, trying to conceal the angry tone I was so familiar with, pretending to be worried about me as he played the role of the poor husband who had no idea how his wife spent her day.

'No. Isn't she with you?' Even my mom was surprised that I was out that late.

'I went hunting to Ajloun this morning, and when I came back, she wasn't home. She's still not home but her car and car keys are here.'

'That's unlike her. She called me this morning and told me she was going to get her hair done, but I didn't hear from her after that. Did you ask Rawan?'

'Yes, but she doesn't know either.'

'You've got me worried now. It's ten o'clock. Let me try calling Laila and I'll get back to you.'

She tried calling me, but my cell phone didn't ring because it was switched off. I felt her pain. How I wished I still had my voice, still possessed the ability to whisper in her ear and dispel her fears. But even if I could whisper in her ear, what would I say to her? Would I tell her about my death? Or would I let her find out by herself?

I was gutted to realize that I was doomed to following her

around, a silent witness to her fear and agony. I was shaken by the certainty that I was bound to watch her collapse at the idea of living the rest of her life without me and not be able to comfort or console her.

She called Firas back. 'Her phone is switched off, Firas. Any idea where she might be? Did anything happen between you two this morning?'

'No, nothing. She was in bed when I left the house early this morning. I'll go out and look for her now.'

'Where will you go this late?'

'I don't know. The usual places she frequents with her friends.'

'Okay. Swing by and take her dad with you.'

'Is he still awake? Let him sleep. I'll call you as soon as I find her.'

'No. No. He's still up and he's waiting for you. Come.'

Firas got dressed and picked up my dad half an hour later. The two searched for me everywhere I could have been, with no success. They roamed the streets of Amman until sunrise, form Jara Café downtown to Books@Café in Jebel Amman to Blue Fig in Abdoun. They even searched for me at Cozmo and Taj Mall and other places.

In the morning, when they were sure I had disappeared, they called the police.

CHAPTER 7

HE DIDN'T HAVE THE LUXURY TO EXPRESS HIS LOSS

TARIQ

MY corpse was in a dumpster on a side street on Airport Road, but the area where Tariq got rid of my body wasn't completely deserted or remote. That's why it was easy for the police to find me.

An old man helped them. Carrying a black garbage bag filled with empty cans and plastic bottles he had collected to sell to recycling factories, the old man approached the dumpster two days after I died looking for something to salvage. He lowered the bag to the ground and approached the dumpster with caution, careful to avoid being startled by a cat searching for something to eat. What he didn't expect was that his hand, the hand used to the clink of aluminum cans, would land on a human head.

The next day, my mom stood next to my dad listening to a detective explaining how the police found my body inside a dumpster on Airport Road. She reached out and grabbed my dad's shoulder, trying to steady herself, refusing to accept what the detective was saying. She didn't want to believe that the woman the detective was talking about was her only daughter, the center of her life, the core of her happiness. She yelled at him, demanding he showed more professionality, telling him to verify his information before uttering such baseless inconceivable claims.

The detective pulled some photos out of a folder and handed them to my dad, who looked at them silently, tears filling his eyes, before passing them to my mother. When she held the photos, her heart almost stopped. She froze in her place when she saw my face: cold, silenced, dead. It looked paler in the photo, tilted to the right, the way she used to see it at night as I slept in my bed. My eyes were closed, my hair plastered to my face, like a lifeless angel.

She threw the photos at the detective, shaking. 'This is not Laila!' she yelled at him as she burst into tears. 'Not Laila!' she screamed again. 'Not Laila!' She kept on screaming the same words over and over again as though by doing so, she could erase the undeniable fact revealed in the photos.

She took a few steps toward the detective, pushed him fiercely as she screamed, 'Get out! Get out! I don't want to see your face!'

My dad was quick to control the situation. He gathered her in his arms and tried to calm her down. She tried to resist him, kicking and screaming at the detective until she lost her energy and collapsed, her anger turning to agony. My dad turned her to face him. He caressed her hair and held her tightly as she let her tears flow.

Like my mom, Tariq refused to believe I was dead. He seemed to hold onto a parallel universe, an imaginary world in which I was still alive. My image refused to leave him. I took over all his thoughts. I could hear him whisper my name first thing when he opened his eyes in the morning. I could feel him talk to me, asking me to keep him company all day long. At night, before he went to bed, he would go to the bathroom and lock the door behind him, holding a towel and kissing it the way he used to kiss my hand, hugging it close to his chest and whispering to it, 'Good night, Ma'am.' Then he would go back to bed and turn his back to his wife, wishing he could fall into a coma and never wake up again.

But unlike my mom, Tariq didn't have the freedom to

express his loss and put words to his agony; he had to hide his pain from his wife and kids, to wear a smile and fulfill all his duties. He had to wake up in the morning like he always did and avoid looking in the bathroom mirror while shaving, as if he was afraid he would see my face in the mirror. He would turn the shower on and stand under the water for a long time. It might have been the only place where he could let his tears fall freely. After the shower, he would put his suit on and stand in front of the mirror, shaking his head as though he could hear me complimenting his elegant taste. He would pick up his cologne bottle and spray some on his neck and wrists, the way he did for me. Then he would sit at the kitchen table and have his breakfast, eat slowly, careful not to raise his wife's suspicion. Sometimes, he would snap back into reality, and, realizing that his son Qais had asked him a question and was waiting for an answer, try to interact with him and reply. After that, he would head out to his clinic and get busy with his patients.

In the evening, when he came home and his wife Ikram approached him, he tried to interact with her the way he did before. Start and finish the sex act which never satisfied or appealed to him. Play the role required of him, the same boring routine. But, a week after the accident, he realized he couldn't get hard. He no longer could deceive his body or control it the way he did before. When his wife approached him that day for sex, he tried, unsuccessfully. She didn't say anything. Maybe she didn't want to embarrass him. She didn't bother him for a few days and tried again later, unsuccessfully.

Outside the bedroom, Ikram updated Tariq on the last news about my case, which had become the talk of the building and the neighborhood and the entire city. My story became her sole occupation and favorite subject because the crime was so shocking and frightening, especially because the police had not apprehended the perpetrator.

'Tariq, why don't you get someone to change the locks?' she asked him the day after the accident, before he went out to work.

That day, she didn't go back to their house after she picked the kids up from school. Instead, she headed straight to her parents' house and waited until Tariq was done with work for them to go back together. It was like that for a week before she asked her brother, who was a student at the university, to move in with them until the criminal was caught. Tariq, who wasn't especially fond of her brother, had to put up with him and tolerate his intrusive presence.

In a matter of hours, Ikram had become an expert in analyzing and reconstructing crime scenes. She presented Tariq with a new theory every day.

'They say her husband used to hit her,' she said to Tariq. I heard that from one of the neighbors, someone I never even greeted or spoke to even as we ran into each other in the building.

The neighbor Ikram was referring to claimed she heard me and Firas yell at each other almost every day. That was the only correct part of her claim. She also claimed that I never shut up until Firas hit me the way I deserved. That was the false part. Ikram said that Firas probably hit me the day of the incident but never meant to kill me.

'He probably hit her over the head, or pushed her against the wall and banged her head until she died!' She startled Tariq with her detailed ingenious take on what happened to me. She surprised him even more when she fell quiet all of a sudden, going over her own projections of the events, before adding, 'Ah! But that doesn't explain the secret behind removing her body and disposing of it all the way on Airport Road. Whoever killed her must have planned the murder ahead of time.'

'They say she was seeing someone else,' she told him one day.

Tariq's heart almost stopped when Ikram said that. He was angry at the way she talked about me and at the same time terrified his secret had been discovered.

He silenced her right away: 'Ikram, shame on you. This is somebody's honor you're talking about here.'

'They say she wanted to get a divorce but her husband refused. He threatened to take her to marriage court if she left the house,' she said.

'They say she was pregnant,' she said.

'They say a thief broke into the house in the morning and when she tried to catch him, he killed her and got rid of her body,' she said.

'They say whoever killed her was definitely someone close to her, someone she knew for a while. It might even be one of the neighbors,' she said.

Tariq played along with Ikram's theorizing in the beginning, despite his agony, in order not to raise suspicions if he reacted unexpectedly, but her interest in me and my case became an obsession for her. He tried to assure her that there was no need to be afraid, because, deep inside, he knew what happened. He was in bad shape mentally and could hardly put up with Ikram's overdramatic reactions. He tried to steer her toward other theories suggesting the crime was an isolated incident unlikely to happen again in the same neighborhood. He wanted to comfort her and wanted her to stop bothering him. After two weeks had passed, he could no longer tolerate her overblown fear and endless guesswork and demanded she stopped discussing my case with him. He started getting angry and shut her up every time she brought up the subject.

I think she was generally surprised at his calmness, how he seemed to shrug off what happened as if he didn't care

about her and his children and wasn't worried about their
safety. She most definitely noticed that he never locked the
outside door when he left for work in the morning or double-
checked to make sure it was locked before they went to bed
at night. He wasn't concerned about her, she thought. Never
called to check on her and the kids when he stayed out late.
In fact, she never gave him the chance because she called him
every half-hour or so and rushed him back home.

Every night, Tariq would retrace Ikram's steps around the
house, switching off the lights she turned on to keep on to
scare off the thief. When she called her friends, she described
Tariq's way of handling the situation as of someone who didn't
fully fathom the level of danger they were in, or as a natural
reaction of a man who could fully control his nerves, who
refused to let fear paralyze him. She didn't realize that fear
was seeping through him and taking control of his thoughts.
Unlike me, she didn't feel his heart stop every time someone
knocked at the door or his phone rang. She didn't see how he
held his breath when she started filling him in about my case.
Her mind didn't connect the dots between his rising blood
pressure, the persistent headaches he suffered, his inability to
get a hard-on, and the emotional state he was in. She was
seeing him the way she wanted to see him: a mountain. She
didn't sense the volcano boiling inside him, about to erupt.

A volcano which seemed to calm down for a few minutes,
right before she threw the news at him: 'They caught the killer.'
The volcano erupted when she added, 'Her husband Firas.'

Tariq was torn between feeling guilty toward an innocent
man who would be hanged, and his own fear for his life,
his reputation, and his family. But despite that torment, the
hardest and most persistent feelings were the agony of losing
me and missing me, and his shame at how I would have
viewed his cowardly reluctance to come forward to confess

what happened.

He staggered into the bedroom after Ikram told him about Firas, but before he reached his bed, he fell unconscious to the floor.

CHAPTER 8

THE FIRST DAYS OF MY MARRIAGE

FIRAS

I WAS extremely happy during our first days of marriage. My problems with Firas had not started yet. That was before we realized that our sexual incompatibility would ultimately impact our feelings for each other and our marriage. Like any other bride, I was happy to move in with the man I loved and eager to start a family with him, a family like the one I grew up in, based on a healthy relationship, on love and mutual respect.

Although I was stubborn, refusing to let anyone dictate how to act and rejecting anyone who tried to force me to change my habits, still, I thought that marriage was a relationship based on the participation of two people and requiring collaboration from them both. I knew that the success of a marriage was built on honesty, open dialogue, and necessary concessions. I loved my husband when I married him. His peace of mind and happiness were important to me; that's why I avoided direct confrontations with him and ignored his infuriarting attempts to control our relationship.

I didn't object when Firas approached me the day after we came back from our honeymoon, at his parents' house for dinner. He kissed me gently and asked me to button up my shirt. I took that as a romantic gesture, as Firas's way of expressing his love and protection of me. I decided not to blow the incident out of proportion, even though I remembered wearing the same top when we were engaged without him objecting or saying it revealed too much.

Once again, I didn't create any problems when he hugged me a few days after that and whispered in my ear, 'What are you going to feed us tomorrow?' He knew very well that I didn't like cooking. I had warned him before we got married that I had no intention to cook nor did I have any interest in learning.

I turned to him that day, kissed him on the cheek, and said, 'What will *you* feed us?'

He dealt with the situation in a diplomatic way. He knew me very well by then, so he suggested, 'What do you think of us cooking together?'

I didn't object as long as we did that together.

But Firas was shrewd. He let me decide on which dish to make, pretending to show interest in me and my opinion. The next day he woke up early and suggested going to the supermarket himself for groceries. When we started cooking later, he let me handle everything without saying a word. He looked up a recipe for *maqluba* online and held his phone as he dictated the steps to me, without directly showing me that he had delegated the cooking to me. He cut the potatoes and cut the meat, but he did that in a way which suggested he was being a sous chef, a helper, not responsible for the final result. When we were confused about something, he called his mom and asked for help. When we finished cooking, neither he nor I was proud of the outcome. He didn't admit that to me though. Instead, he spooned some of the rice with a bit of yogurt and a piece of meat and pretended to be astonished at how good the food tasted, saying, 'Hmmmm. Thank you. It's delicious.'

I humored him. I didn't insist that the food didn't taste good. Didn't say the rice was overcooked and the meat undercooked. And I didn't tell him it was the first and last time I would try to cook.

I think that neither one of us was ready for married life or prepared for what that life entailed. Firas entered into it with the same notions he witnessed growing up in the relationship between his parents. I entered it with a different mentality based on how I saw my parents live and treat each other. Although it was normal to split tasks between any two people based on the desires and abilities of each one, dividing them on a gender basis and putting all housework on me because I was a woman provoked me.

During the first days of our marriage, I felt as if I had moved to a new work environment and had become the responsibility of a manager who had no prior experience in management. Describing marriage as work and Firas as a manager might sound a bit exaggerated. I don't want to do him injustice. He wasn't bossy, not before we got married and not after, but his view of masculinity was clear in the way he treated me and imposed it on me. For him, masculinity was a role he had to automatically play without thinking. As a man, he believed that he held a superior position in his family and was directly responsible for it. He believed that everything about me, be it the way I acted or dressed or talked, reflected on him and on his manhood. That's why he allowed himself to direct me and didn't hesitate to tell me to do what he believed was a duty I had to fulfill.

It bothered me how the deciding factor between us was now our gender. I detested that strange distinction which drew an inverse relationship between the freedoms I enjoyed in the past and between Firas's idea of how they affected his manhood. Things didn't stop at household chores which Firas had automatically abandoned but surpassed that to include otherwise insignificant matters which led to our first fight.

I remember him insisting we take his car instead of mine every time we wanted to go out and demanding to be the one who drove. I found it strange, but I said nothing at first, not until he surprised me one day by refusing my suggestion that we take my car and I drive. He gave me a snide look and argued that his car was better than mine, even though my car was not that bad. When I asked him to let me drive his car, since he insisted we take it, he pretended he didn't hear me. I repeated my offer clearly, stressing my words, leaving no room for him to pretend not to hear me. He replied jokingly, 'No. I don't trust women drivers.'

I didn't like his joke. He hadn't really refused my offer because he didn't trust women drivers. That I knew. He refused because he was embarrassed to let his wife drive while he was in the car. It was a simple situation not worth fighting over, but I found myself snapping back, 'Fine. And I don't trust men drivers.' Adding, 'Let's go in two cars then.'

He finally relented and let me drive but grumbled and shifted in his seat the entire way. Shortly after we were on the road, he found a way to drive from the passenger seat. He had a comment every time a car tried to pass me. 'Take the right lane. Let him pass.' When I reached the first intersection, he said, 'This is a dangerous intersection. Drive slower. Put your signal on.' When a car merged in my lane suddenly and almost hit me, he yelled, 'What a jackass! Honk at him!'

I started feeling anxious then because his comments confused me and I no longer knew how to focus on driving, so I raised my voice angrily at him: 'Can you stop talking and let me drive?'

That kept him quiet the entire way. In fact, he was so upset that he didn't talk to me for the rest of the day.

And that's how it went. Firas would try to project and impose himself as the one who knew more about life, but I never accepted that. Nor did I keep quiet. It was a matter of time before I started arguing with him, debating him, and standing up to him, regardless of how small or big the issue at hand. And with that, our problems started to metastasize.

To make things worse, as he failed to impose himself on me personally, he tried more and more to impose himself sexually. He might have thought, naively, that by acting rough in bed, he would force me to obey him outside the bedroom too, but that only succeeded in shutting me off emotionally and sexually. At first, I tried to stay calm and suppress my desire to take control when we had sex, so he wouldn't get upset the way he did on our wedding night. But I literally lost it one day when he tightened his grip around my wrists and hurt me as he penetrated me in a rough way, unlike the previous times we had sex. My body shook with anger and I yelled at him and asked to stop.

He stopped right away, apologized, and tried to smooth things over, but I was repulsed and didn't want to continue. After that, I stopped wanting to have sex with him. I became an expert in finding excuses to avoid it. And, as I avoided him sexually and our problems grew, our passion ultimately died. We stopped being intimate. Stopped kissing and holding hands. All the warmth and love from our dating and engagement days evaporated into thin air.

CHAPTER 9

IF I WERE HIM, I WOULD COOK AND WASH AND CLEAN FOR YOU

TARIQ

I **FLOAT** around Tariq's bed on the ICU floor. I approach him and touch his hand. He feels my presence and opens his eyes and smiles, murmuring a few words which Ikram doesn't understand. She is standing at the foot of his bed. She doesn't see me and can't feel my presence just as Tariq isn't aware of her and doesn't realize she's there. But I, in my postmortem state, can see and feel both of them.

Under the effect of anesthesia, Tariq is in between two worlds, mine and hers. He has been closer to mine the second he struggled to catch his breath and his blood pressure went up just before he fell in the bedroom.

I understand what he whispers: '*Laila.*' He adds in a weak voice, 'Welcome, Ma'am,' as if he is recalling the first time I visited him in his clinic.

That day, we were messaging on WhatsApp when he asked me about my location. I happened to be crossing Abdoun Bridge on my way to visit a friend who lived in Jebel Amman, close to Tariq's clinic on the 4th Circle. He asked me to stop by. Unlike the previous times, I accepted readily because I wanted to finally see him after months of texts. The idea of going to see a doctor in his clinic and subduing him was a fantasy of mine which excited me to no end. On top of that, it felt safer to meet a stranger – despite all our messages – in a public space.

When I arrived, his clinic was full, but he didn't let me wait. He came out to greet me and escort me to his office the second his secretary informed him of my arrival. I extended my hand to shake his and felt an immediate spark when we touched. He greeted me warmly and stood by the door of his office saying audibly, 'Welcome, Ma'am.' He said it in front of everyone, in the same respectful tone used by Jordanian men to greet women, not in the submissive tone he used during our chats.

I walked in front of him, filled with desire.

He looked more handsome than his photos suggested. His deep voice and position as a doctor added another dimension to the dynamics of our relationship. The fact that he was a dad left me with the impression that he was an independent and successful man. His masculinity seemed natural and complete in his white coat, unlike Firas, who was at home that moment. Firas who made me feel he was no more than a boy trying to play the role of a man.

Even though the dictates of social hierarchy favored Tariq, and even though I felt like a little girl in front of him, for I was in my late twenties and he in his early forties, I maintained my self-confidence and felt an overwhelming desire to prove that those differences meant nothing for us. I felt a bit of awe for what he stood for, a man who possessed all the qualities society glorified, but I straightened my back and sat in front of him, equal to equal.

Seeing him like in his clinic added to my attraction to him. Something inside me conceded that having a man with all those traits was a challenge to my femininity and a chance to fulfill myself in a way I never had before. The awe easily dissipated when Tariq started talking. His words were honest and his voice warm and endearing. I felt like I was sitting with a childhood friend, someone I had known all my life, not a man I had only connected with by sexting online.

We talked that day, the usual talk, like any man and woman meeting for the first time and trying to get to know each other. In Tariq's his clinic that day, there was no room for sex talk, despite the two of us being aware that sex was what brought us together in the first place. It hovered there in the air, and like any conversation between a man and a woman connected by strong desire, it pulsated in our looks and the tone of our voices, colored the lines between our unspoken words.

The second I lay my eyes on Tariq, I wanted him to be submissive to me, and that's why I was quick to steer our conversation in the direction I wanted. In turn, he was quick to show that he was interested in me and eager to please me. For instance, when he said, 'The weather is nice today,' I replied, 'No, it's not. I'm feeling warm.' When he ordered me coffee and it tasted bitter, I didn't hesitate to let him know.

He was quick to ask, 'They didn't add sugar for you?'

I replied gruffly, 'No. They didn't.'

I noticed a framed photo of an adolescent boy on his desk the moment I entered his clinic. I suspected it was a photo of his son. I gathered enough courage to point at the photo and ask him, 'Your son?'

I hoped he would deny it and tell me it was his nephew, but he replied, 'Yup. That's Qais, heir to the throne.'

I hid my disappointment and looked at his fingers searching for something to assure me he wasn't married. He wasn't wearing a ring, so I asked him, to make sure, 'Married?'

He answered me quietly and in an embarrassed tone, 'Yes, I am.'

We were silent for a second before I confessed: 'So am I.' I added after another short silence, 'I asked him for a divorce a week ago.'

I waited for him to tell me he was ready to divorce his wife or that he was planning to do that in the future, but he didn't say anything. I asked him about his son, 'How old is Qais?'

'Twelve years.'

'Sweet.'

I picked up the frame and studied the photo. 'He looks like you,' I said as I put it back. 'Do you have more kids?'

'Yes. Mira and Salam. Mira is ten and Salam the baby is three,' he said proudly.

'Mashallah,' I said, surprised, before adding sarcastically, 'Any more on the way?'

He laughed and said, 'No,' then asked me in turn, 'What about you?'

'No. Thank God. I don't have kids.'

I have to admit that even though I was disappointed that he had kids, that very fact intensified my attraction to him, completing his image as man in my mind. But that day, as we talked, I made a decision to end our relationship before it developed into something more serious.

'Where do you live?' He asked me.

'Sweifieh. Behind Cozmo.'

'It's a nice area. I'm looking for an apartment there myself.'

'What are you looking for?'

'A big apartment. Four bedrooms. But it's hard to find a place that big.'

I didn't consider the ramifications when I answered him quickly, 'You'll find one. There's an apartment in my building.'

'Really? On the ground floor?' He asked.

'No, we have the ground floor apartment. There is one on the second floor. Here. Call this number and inquire about it.'

I picked my phone and looked for the owner's number. I waited for Tariq to switch his phone so I could read the number to him.

'Where do you work, Laila?'

'I'm a customer-relations manager at Arab Bank.'

'Great! I might need a home loan for the apartment. How's the loan business these day at the bank?'

'Stop by whenever you're ready and I'll draw the papers for you. Don't worry.'

He winked as he added, 'I'm sure everyone stands at attention for you at the bank?'

'And outside the bank,' I replied quickly.

He changed the subject and asked me, 'What does your husband do?'

'He worked in marketing, but he quit his job a while ago and he's home now.'

'I bet you he cleans and cooks for you,' he said in a sly tone.

'Nope! He doesn't do anything. He can hardly manage feeding himself.'

'If I were him, I would clean and cook and wash for you. I would do anything you wish, Ma'am.'

I laughed and asked, as I steered the conversation in a different direction without entirely avoiding the subject, 'Do you know how to cook?'

'I know how to make a mean omelet and sizzling shakshouka.'

'Omelet and shakshouka? Both?' I asked, sarcastically. 'I don't like either one.'

'In that case, I'll learn how to make another dish for you. As long as you're happy with me.'

'Sure.'

'How about you? What do you like to cook?'

'I don't cook,' I replied.

I felt his shock, but he said, 'Someone like you is not supposed to cook.' Then he asked after he thought more realistically about my life with Firas, 'But how do you guys manage? Eating at restaurants?'

'Yup, either restaurants or sandwiches or living on my mom's and his mom's cooking.'

'I'm sure their cooking is delicious, but when we become neighbors, I'll ask Ikram to bring you food every day,' he said jokingly.

'As long as you're the one who cooks it,' I said, winking at him.

'Your wish is my command, Ma'am.'

I felt my heart skip a beat. It was hard to breathe. I put my hand on my chest and tried to take a deep breath.

'Are you all right?' He asked.

I was tempted to ignore it. Shortness of breath was no big deal to me. I was used to it every now and then. But then I remembered I was with a doctor, so I decided to ask him for a consultation. 'I don't know, doctor. Sometimes I feel shortness of breath and my heart starts beating in a strange way.'

'How long has this been going on?'

'For some time.'

'What do you feel? Pain in your chest? How often does it happen?'

'Yes, a little pain. I'm not sure. I used to have it spaced out before but now I feel that it's happening every few days.'

'Do you feel dizzy?'

'Not all the time.'

'I don't think there is any reason to worry. Let's do an EKG, just to make sure.'

'But I have to leave now. Let's do that another day.' I picked up my purse and looked for my car keys and sunglasses in it as I got ready to leave.

'As you wish, Ma'am. Would you like me to book you an appointment tomorrow?' he said as he walked me to the door.

'I'll confirm with you later,' I replied, ready to leave.

He came close to me before opening the door, raised my hand to his lips and kissed it. 'We're at your service, Ma'am,' he said while gazing into my eyes.

I didn't withdraw my hand. I let him hold it longer than expected so he would kiss it another time. I wanted to leave him with the impression that I was the one in control, not him.

I left his clinic without turning to look back. Every part of my body was asserting the fact that Tariq was my knight in shining armor. The man every girl dreamed of. A man whose mere presence made me feel the kind of comfort I never felt before.

But societal norms called for something else. Danger bells were ringing, dictating I should leave him. I had already broken so many taboos by asserting my sexual desires and having enough courage to ask Firas for a divorce regardless of the consequences. But still, I wasn't ready to fall in love with a married man who was the father of three children.

I left him that day filled with a longing not unlike the feeling coursing through me now as I hover around his bed.

I was hard on myself and on him. I stopped replying to his messages and ignored his calls, until he surprised me one day by knocking on my office door at the bank.

I remember the look in his eyes. I remember the longing in them, so evident when he entered and addressed me as any stranger there to apply for loan. He was powerless then as he is today, lying on a hospital bed, trying to reach out and touch me.

I reach out and entwine my fingers with his. I let him

pull my hand to him and kiss it the way he did on our first meeting. But today, I don't withdraw it as I move closer and hug his head. As much as I want to pull him and take him with me to my new world, I know it isn't time for him to leave. Not yet.

I kiss his forehead and wish him a speedy recovery.

I let the brief moment which has united us vanish peacefully like the other beautiful moments we once had.

CHAPTER 10

WHAT'S THAT MASCULINITY HE'S TALKING ABOUT?

FIRAS

FIRAS is in total shock when the police start interrogating him as a prime suspect in my case. He isn't prepared to defend himself properly. All signs point to our shaky relationship. Testimonies from our friends, families, and neighbors confirm that it was bad, and there is precedence and proof of the verbal and physical abuse I had suffered in the last months. He doesn't cooperate with the police. Instead, he squirms in his seat and acts nervous when he suspects the detective is accusing him of killing me.

'So where were you the day of the crime?' the detective asks.

The answer is simple. He was in Ajloun, but he went there alone. The only proof of his trip is the three birds he has in the freezer. Also, the time of his return is so close to the time of the crime, but, and because Firas is nervous and irritated, he can't remember the exact time of his return. Add to that the Firas is used to lying and exaggerating. He tells the detective he came back around two in the afternoon, even though he was back at twelve noon.

Ikram is standing at her bedroom window when Firas arrives from Ajloun. Fifteen minutes have passed since her husband left from the back door. She doesn't see him, but she notices Firas coming back, because when she sees him park his car, she thinks that Tariq has forgotten something and is back to get it. When the detective asks her, she isn't precise. She says she saw Firas enter his house at eleven o'clock or a few minutes past that.

'But your neighbor saw you come into your house much earlier,' the detective says to Frias without breaking eye contact.

Firas doesn't like the accusing tone. 'Earlier than that?' he asks, incredulous.

'She saw you at ten thirty,' the detective changes the time, making it look earlier to irritate Firas.

'No way it was ten thirty. It might have been twelve or one, but definitely not before.'

'You just said you arrived at two,' the detective says, raising his eyebrows.

'Are you trying to make me slip, man? I meant at noon. I didn't notice the exact time.' Firas says, trying to control his temper.

The detective keeps quiet for some time before approaching Firas and examining his forehead. 'And what's this scratch on your forehead?'

The question takes Firas by surprise. He touches his forehead and answers, 'From a tree branch. It happened when I was hunting in Ajloun.'

'Do you have a hunting license?'

'Yes, I do.'

The detective touches the scar on Firas's arm left by the cut I caused when I threw the frame at him a couple of days before. He asks in a provoking tone, 'And this one is from a tree branch too?'

As usual, Firas is fast to lie without thinking: 'No. I fell off a rock while out hunting.'

'And that fall broke your phone screen too?' the detective asks. He smiles as he holds Firas's keychain with the smiling face charm and flips it between his fingers before asking, in a sly tone, 'Did you ever hit Laila?'

Firas looks at his interrogator in a strange way before answering, 'No.'

'Her mom says you threw your phone at her two days before she disappeared and that you wished she was dead.'

Firas's jaw drops in shock. He is about to lose his temper. He answers firmly, 'I didn't throw it at her. I threw it at the wall after she provoked me.'

'Provoked you? And how did she provoke you?'

It's Firas's chance to gain the detective's sympathy. They are both men. The detective will certainly understand the shame that would stick to a man who can't prevent his wife from leaving the house and has no power to ask her where she is going. Firas is quick to answer the detective, letting his displeasure from what he is about to say color the tone of his voice. 'She wanted to leave the house without my permission,' he says in a deep voice, faking anger.

It appears that the new revelation has the desired effect on the detective, who changes his tone and asks calmly, 'So you threw the phone at her?'

'Not at her. At the wall. She provoked me.'

'Well, if Laila didn't obey you and she asked you for a divorce, why not divorce her and live in peace?' The detective then asks, 'Do you love her?'

I expect Firas to say that he doesn't love me anymore, that he wants to humiliate me in court before divorcing me, but I am surprised when he controls himself and replies, pretending to be sad: 'Yes. I love her.'

The detective adjusts his posture, a sly smile on his face. 'You love her despite the fact that she hit you?'

I didn't really hit him, and he wouldn't dare raise his hand at me. In fact, I wouldn't categorize our fights and violence toward each other as assault. We didn't have a healthy relationship, I admit, but who among us can avoid marital problems? Who among us can skirt around those problems all the time and keep them from becoming verbal altercations or developing into one form of violence or another?

Firas had a fiery temper and I wasn't an angel. I was used to fighting for my rights and not allowing anyone to slight me. Firas's temper didn't scare me. I met his bursts of anger with worse bursts to intimidate him and force him to back down. Most of the time, he was wise enough to let go when he realized that I was ready to burn everything to the ground. So, the number of times things exploded and reached physical violence between us were few.

'No, she didn't hit me,' Firas replies, quite irritated.

'Are you sure?' the detective asks.

'Yes, I'm sure,' Firas says firmly.

But the detective is also sure of what he means. He pulls out the police report Firas had taken out against me the month before and hands it to Firas, before pulling it out of Firas's momentarily hand and reading it out loud:

"I, the undersigned, Firas Salam, want to register an official complaint against my wife Laila Salam, for attacking me physically and pushing me hard against the glass kitchen door, causing it to smash in my hands. The attached medical report reveals that the impact had caused severe damage to my left hand and shows tear of nerve tissue sustained as a result of glass particles penetrating the skin and reaching the nerves."

The detective stops reading and looks Firas in the eye. Firas starts sweating. 'She pushed me that day while I had my back turned and I fell on the glass door and it broke in my hands,' he says.

'Shame on you. A man doesn't report his wife,' the detective says. 'And why did she push you?'

I pushed him when I didn't succeed in getting back my cell phone from him after he snatched it as I was complaining to Rawan about his neglect and sloppiness. It happened seconds after he and I had a verbal altercation.

That day, I came home at eight o'clock after a long tiring day at work and I wasn't in a good mood. Seeing Firas busy playing a football game on the PlayStation, unconcerned about the messy state the house was in, provoked me.

Firas was in a weird place mentally, having been jobless for a year. I think that being emotionally detached from him and telling him to stop asking me for sex, as well as asking for a divorce, wounded him deeply, shook his view of his masculinity and manhood. I didn't care about that. What was this masculinity he talked about and was obsessed with? The masculinity he tried to impose in bed, which grossed me out? Or his inflated macho ego which he used to justify his failures? Or the masculinity his mother had instilled in him, leaving him lazy and unable to do the simplest chores?

Firas quit his job after an argument with his boss. He refused to concede and accept his position as inferior to her, with the excuse that his masculinity was hurt. He adamantly refused to sign up for any other job which didn't satisfy his ego.

He was used to throwing his clothes on the floor or the couch in the living room, or on the chair in the bedroom without any sense of responsibility. When I asked him to put them back in the closet, he would stall, get irritated, and try to find a way to avoid doing that. Only when I insisted and raised my voice would he concede, pick up his clothes as though they were a pile of trash, ball them, and throw them into the closet.

He never understood that his clothes needed to be washed unless I smelled their stinky odor on him and asked him to change. He never cared where he put his shoes, be it by the main door or in the living room, the kitchen or the bedroom. And when it came to laundry, doing the dishes, and cooking, he wanted nothing to do with any of that, as if he were a spoiled kid. He was unwilling to admit he was a grown-up man, obligated to at least learn the most basic tasks to take care of himself. Whenever I asked him to do any of the tasks men did, like buying groceries for the house or changing the gas cylinder, I had to write him a list. I had to tolerate his huffing and puffing before he would bring himself to get dressed and head to the supermarket. Once at the supermarket, he would call me repeatedly to ask which brand of shampoo or soap to buy when he couldn't find the ones we were used to. And when he came back, he would leave the bags on the counter for me put the groceries away. When it came to the gas cylinder, he would delay and find every excuse not to do it, until I eventually gave up and called the janitor to change it for us.

The same applied to Tuesdays, when the cleaning lady came to tidy up the house. Firas had no clue how to supervise her work, so he would call me with any questions or requests she had, regardless of how simple they were. He would try to leave the house when she was there to avoid the noise from the vacuum cleaner and the need to move from his place when she had to mop the floor or move the furniture. He spent most of his time at home after losing his job, but still, he never changed the way he acted or tried to take on some of the chores. In fact, he became lazier and messier.

When I came home that evening, the living room smelled nauseating, like a mixture of his dirty socks and the Big Mac cheeseburger he had eaten a few hours before. As usual, he hadn't bothered to clean up and throw away the food wrappers. He left the Pepsi cup on the table, moisture seeping from its base and mixing with half-eaten pieces of french fries and empty salt and ketchup packets. He had his legs stretched on the table and was focused on his next move on the PlayStation when he heard me yell at him, 'You're such a slob, Firas. Why is the house like this, for heaven's sake?'

Firas waited until he lost the penalty kick on the game before he hit the pause button and set the controller aside. He stared at me angrily. 'Respect yourself and don't raise your voice!'

'How am I supposed to respect myself when you don't respect yourself and can't see the mess around you and smell your own stench?' I answered as I opened the windows to air the room. 'Move! Put your socks in the laundry and clean the table.'

'When this half is finished,' he answered, ignoring me and restarting the game.

My blood boiled. He thought he could simply dismiss me and go back to his game, but I wasn't going to let him continue playing and leave the house in the mess he created. And because he provoked me, I wanted to provoke him too. I didn't hesitate to approach the TV and switch it off.

He threw a vengeful look at me as if I had killed someone dear to him. He threw the controller to the side, raised his forefinger in my face, and yelled, 'Are you nuts? Did you lose your mind? Don't you dare do that again! Do you understand?' Saying that, he picked up the Pepsi cup, threw it on the floor, and pushed the table with his foot. 'I told you I will clean up when this half is over, but now, to teach you a lesson, I won't! There!' With one move, he swept the food wrappers to the floor. 'Let's see now who's going to clean up!' he yelled, heading to the bedroom and slamming the door behind him.

I followed him and opened the door, screaming at him, 'You're going to clean up and you're going to clean up now.'

'I told you I won't. Leave me alone now before I raise hell.'

But I didn't leave him. I stood my ground and repeated, 'Get up and clean your mess. I won't leave you until you do.'

Enraged, he started shaking and approached me so fast I thought he wanted to hit me, but instead, he clenched his fist and punched the door. 'For the last time, Laila, leave me alone!' He left the room and went to the guest bathroom.

That was when I called Rawan. I was so angry. I didn't care if he heard me or not: 'He's such a slob, Rawan. He spent the entire day playing games on the PlayStation. You should see the mess in the house. It's like a tornado just passed through it.'

'He's a loser. All his life, he's been a loser.'

'I don't want anyone to tell me to be patient and not to divorce him.'

As soon as I said that, he appeared and snatched the phone from my hand. He had it with him as he went toward the glass door leading to the balcony. I was afraid he was going to throw my phone outside. I followed him as he was about to open the door and grabbed his T-shirt to try and force him to stop, to give me back my phone. The fabric of the T-shirt ripped from the force of my grip. After that happened, he pushed me violently, turned his back to me, opened the door, and made as if to throw the phone, screaming, '*No phone for you!*'

At that moment, I had no other way of retrieving my phone before he threw it but to push him with all my might toward the door. I didn't know I had the strength to shove him with such force and didn't expect him to fall so easily. It's possible that the way he was standing, ready to throw the phone, had caused him to lose his balance. As he did, his body swayed and hit the glass door, which crashed to the floor.

And on top of it, Firas.

Glass scattered everywhere and some fragments pierced Firas's arms, face, and neck. I rushed to help him stand up without really knowing what else to do. He was screaming from the pain and hurling insults at me, but I ignored him. I rushed to the kitchen, grabbed a napkin, and carefully cleaned his blood before helping him get in my car. I drove him to the hospital. Not for a second did I think that he would tell the doctor what had actually happened. I was surprised when he insisted on reporting the incident to the police.

That day, I left him at the hospital and didn't go back home. I headed to my parents' house and stayed there for a week. That night, I made up my mind to leave him. I wasn't going to let anyone dissuade me or change my mind, but he came with his parents after a few days and they tried to fix things between us. He apologized because of what happened and said he was ready to drop the complaint if I went back to him. I didn't want to continue living with Firas, but at the same time, I wasn't ready to go to court and face a possible prison sentence. So, I reluctantly agreed to go back to him, but I was determined to leave him as soon as I could.

Here he is now, telling the detective how I pushed him, adding different details, leaving out some, particularly the part about his laziness, sloppiness, and filth. He tells the detective he heard me trash him on the phone and that led him to grab the phone from my hand. He says he was about to throw it out onto the street when I surprised him from the back and pushed him against the glass door.

The detective listens to Firas's story until the end and seems content in the way it turned out. He has just confirmed that there was clear and undeniable violence between Firas and me. The way the detective sees it, matters eventually escalated between us in a way that ended with my murder.

Before the detective ends his interrogation, he takes a plastic bag from a drawer and puts it on the desk in front of

Firas. 'Is this the phone you wanted to throw away?'

Firas recognizes my phone but doesn't understand what the detective is hinting at.

The detective looks at Firas for a long time before he throws a bomb at him. 'We found the phone under your car the day of the crime, which, as I see it, is proof that Laila left the house with you that day.'

The detective takes the phone out of the plastic bag and switches it on. He searches for Firas's name. He locates a voice message Firas left me a month before. He had had too much to drink that night and was angry at me because I was out late and had missed his repeated calls.

'*You know, Laila. The best solution is for me is to shoot you and shoot myself.*'

His voice in the audio sounds calculated and calm, as if he is actually contemplating carrying out his threat. I didn't take the threat seriously though because I knew Firas's words were empty. But the detective doesn't know Firas well. Because of my disappearance and death and the prevailing assumption that I was killed, Firas's verbal threat is incriminating and can't be ignored.

'Why did you kill your wife, Firas?' the detective calmly asks.

Firas's jaw drops.

CHAPTER 11

IF ONLY HE WAS LESS MACHO WITH ME

FIRAS

MY relationship with Firas started deteriorating a few months after our wedding. Once the honeymoon was over, we became more critical of each other, more vocal in expressing our dissatisfaction and distaste. It was clear to me that we viewed marriage differently. Our opposing views widened the rift between us and worsened our problems. It wasn't long before I lost respect for Firas and started thinking seriously of divorce.

I am not referring here to our sexual relationship, which, although unsatisfactory, was not open to discussion at that time and had not become one of my main concerns. Not yet. My status as Firas's wife was a bone of contention between us. According to him, I was expected to be the wife who fulfilled all duties and assumed all house chores and responsibilities an Arab woman was supposed to, including taking care of her husband the way his mother did, even if the wife had a full-time job and her salary was as good as his or higher.

As my objections grew and I remained adamant that we split the responsibilities, Firas became more stubborn, stood his ground, and intensified his sharp criticism of me. His refusal to do the dishes was final, as was his refusal to do the laundry and cook. After a big argument one day, he surprised me with a suggestion which he thought would suit him well. 'Let's get a maid,' he said offhandedly as he finished eating, stacking his dirty dishes in the sink. 'I'll pay for one,' he added while pouring a glass of water.

I didn't like the idea of having a maid in the house. We didn't have children and didn't really need a maid. We demanded little in terms of our upkeep, and our apartment wasn't big enough to accommodate or require a live-in maid. On top of that, I wasn't ready to have a third person living with us. But I didn't object. *If that's what he wants, so be it*, I thought.

We started the process of getting a maid, but Firas lost his job in the meantime. Being unemployed meant he wouldn't be able to afford a maid. I couldn't pay for one myself, so we abandoned the idea, but that didn't ameliorate or solve the differences between us. Losing his job and spending long stretches of time at home didn't change Firas's idea about our presumed social roles. Balancing his imagined masculinity with the requirements of his current life was out of the question for him. Too bad for him, his wife wasn't willing to spoil him and was not ready to carry all the responsibilities alone.

I would have been nicer to him, more understanding and accommodating had it not been for his chauvinistic, macho way of behaving. It would have been different had he not been so backward-thinking, had he stopped linking everything in our relationship to him being a man and me being a woman. Staying at home did not make him less of a man and my success at work did not make me grow a moustache.

Had he been a man with a different mindset, we would have willingly split my salary and ridden out the storm together. He would have felt better spending his time and energy on a useful hobby, carrying house responsibilities without complaining. That would have made him more of a man in my eyes, not less. I find the modern man who is open-minded and confident in himself more attractive than one so burdened by culture that he is more suitable for life in the Stone Age than in twenty-first century Amman.

That being said, I don't expect traditional roles—sexual or otherwise—to be swapped completely between men and women. I believe in gender equality. I believe people are different with diverse desires and needs and inclinations. Not all women are sexually subjugated, nor do all of them aspire to become dominatrices like me. The same applies to men. There are strong and weak men. Describing them as either controlling or subjugated, strong or weak, is wrong. Those characteristics are common between men and women just like any other characteristics and traits. Couples need to appreciate those differences; embrace their individual needs; and be considerate of their sexual, mental, and social compatibility. I also think that other personal characteristics are distributed among individuals in a similar fashion. Women are not necessarily good at cooking. Some women might like it while others hate it. The same applies to doing the laundry, mopping the floor, and fixing the car. All these are tasks which would suit certain people and not others, regardless of their gender.

I won't deny it: my sexual preferences went against the widespread view about women. They pushed me to think differently, to question everything I had been taught about women all my life. Women were not weaker than men but were in fact stronger and more determined. I didn't witness that in all women around me. Most of them believed they were the weaker sex. In fact, they liked the idea and embraced it without feeling embarrassed by its ramifications. It provoked me to no end when those women brought their beliefs to public discussion boards and preached the absolute superiority of men. At the office once, when we discussed men hitting their wives, the opinion of some of the girls astonished me. They had no issue with a wife being physically punished by her husband if she had wronged him. What really surprised me was how one of them laughed, admitting she found the idea of a husband's chastisement and corporal punishment "arousing".

I had no issue with my colleague feeling turned on by the idea of masochism. She had every right to practice that with her significant other. But she had no right to issue a blanket approval for men to hit their wives. That day, I wondered out loud if there were men who felt turned on by their wives physically hurting them. I realized we were incapable of separating our sexual desires from our innermost needs. I imagined how life would have been had the sexual roles Tariq and I played spilled into our daily lives and were manifested outside the bedroom. That most definitely would have gone against my idea of equality between the two sexes. But still, I couldn't deny the fact that those innermost desires, whether we negated them or owned them, were key to the way we thought and they had a big role in forming our views of ourselves.

I, with my mental maturity and life experiences, learned to make a distinction. The contrast between the social role our culture wanted to impose on me as a woman and my sexual preferences was vast. It was a big part of my identity. That's why I became a vocal advocate for women's rights and active participant in the feminist movement demanding gender equality.

My stance on gender equality provoked Firas. I remember the first time I asked him for a divorce. It happened after I took part in a feminist human chain march in the height of the Arab Spring uprisings. Organized by four Jordanian feminist movements under the slogan *"I'M JUST LIKE YOU"*, the march aimed to assert women's status as equal citizens to men with the same rights and duties. At the time, calls for change reached unprecedented highs in Jordan. Women had to raise their voices and demand their rights along the voices calling for political reform, social justice, and an end to corruption.

I believed in the message of the four participating movements: *"Where We Stand"* sought to put an end to honor crimes; *"Mush Shatara"* protested sexual harassment; *"My Mother Is Jordanian and I Have the Right to Have Her Nationality"* demanded equality in passing on nationality rights between the two sexes; and *"Abolish Article 308"* called to repeal a law allowing a rapist to marry his victim and avoid punishment.

That day I wore a white T-shirt and a pair of jeans. Coincidentally, I had just put highlights in my hair the day before. As I was leaving the house in the morning, Firas looked me up and down.

'Are you sure you're going to march on the streets with your friends looking like this?' he asked in a provocative tone.

'Absolutely,' I replied, shrugging off his sarcastic question.

I headed to the march filled with purpose and hope. I was proud of the bold women and men whose activism and courage inspired me and others to join a movement. We carried signs with revolutionary slogans. I chose a sign ridiculing Article 308: *RAPE AND GET MARRIED FOR FREE!* I stood next to 220 young activists, creating a long human chain stretching form Al Dakhylia Circle to Sport City Circle. People passing us responded in the beginning, their curiosity piqued by the slogans on the signs. They stopped and asked us about the slogans and march and applauded our courage. But by noon, the same riffraff who frequented the streets of Amman started harassing us with nasty comments.

We didn't want our human chain to transform from a peaceful act demanding rights to a fight with a band of young men who clearly lacked manners and purpose, so we didn't respond to their provocation. Instead, we channeled all our energy into carrying out our plan and delivering our message. But sadly, what took place on the streets was nothing compared to what happened on news sites and social-media platforms. The macho society we lived in painted our demands as a moral scandal. The female activists asking for social justice for women were described as loose women asking for what was against norms and tradition. Our image was slandered. The words on the signs we carried were photoshopped. Profane comments and insults against us and our families filled the Internet.

Firas just about lost his mind when he found a photo of me on a Facebook page. The words on the slogan I carried were clearly photoshopped to read: DO ME A FAVOR AND RAPE ME. The Facebook post had over one thousand humiliating comments and an equal number of shares. The result was a deliberate attempt to slander me and sabotage my reputation throughout the entire country.

(1)

IF YOU HAD A REAL MAN, YOU WOULN'T HAVE LEFT THE HOUSE LOOKING LIKE THAT.

(2)

WHORE!

(3)

COME ON SWEETY & LET ME RAPE YOU. I PROMISE YOU'LL LIKE IT.

(4)

I WON'T ONLY DO YOU A FAVOR ONCE I GET A CHANCE TO PUT MY HANDS ON YOU. I'LL DO YOUR FAMILY A FAVOR.

(5)

HER HUSBAND IS DEFINITELY A CUCKOLD.

(6)

IF I WERE HER BROTHER, I WOULD HAVE BURIED HER BEFORE SHE STEPPED OUT ON THE STREET.

The rest of the comments were a variation of the same theme.

When I went home after the march, I wasn't aware of the photo or the comments. But I was angry at the ugliness of the detracting calls from the mob of macho men on the street. I needed Firas to stand by me, to support me and make me feel better in my moment of vulnerability. I didn't expect him to greet me by yelling and hurling insults at me as if he were one of those strange ugly men outside and not my husband.

'Happy now?' he attacked me as soon as I walked in the door. 'Did you fulfill your fantasy?'

I ignored him. I headed to the bedroom but he followed me.

'Didn't I tell you there was no need to go?'

'Leave me alone, Firas.' I didn't have the desire or energy to confront him.

'Leave you alone?' he screamed. 'Have you lost your mind? Your photo is everywhere! Did you see it? Did you read the comments?'

I looked at him angrily, shocked at his words. 'Why are you talking to me like this?'

'Why am I talking to you like this? How do you want me to talk to you after you stigmatized all of us? Do you want me to clap for you?' he added, clapping. 'Is that what you want? You want me to tell you bravo and congratulate you for humiliating us? Or should I feel great about the comments from men who want to rape you and those who say you don't have a husband to control you?'

'They're pigs, Firas. Just ignore them,' I replied.

'Just ignore them, heh? Did you forget you're married? Or do you only think of yourself?'

'No, I didn't forget, but I expect my husband to stand by my side and support me, not attack me.'

'No! I'm not going to stand by you or support you when you're wrong. You have to know how to behave and respect your husband and your family.'

My rising anger choked me. I felt my throat tighten. I didn't want to reply, but he continued to provoke me: 'You can't go on another march again.'

Although I had no intention of participating in any more marches or demonstrations or human chains after what happened that morning, Firas's tone and the way he thought he could tell me what to do and not to do were just unacceptable.

'It's not up to you,' I retorted. 'I can do whatever I want.'

'Yes, it's up to me,' he said, his eyes sparkling with cold hatred.

'No, it's not,' I said calmly, sizing him up.

'Fine. I'll tell your dad and we'll see what happens,' he threatened.

'Tell whoever you want. It's not up to you and it will never be up to you,' I shrugged my shoulders, emphasizing my words. Then, I took a deep breath and said, 'Just go ahead and divorce me, Firas. I'm tired of you.'

He left the room without replying. He didn't talk to me for a week afterwards. By that time, the story had lost its fervor and was put behind us. He ended up apologizing to me and we made up.

CHAPTER 12

WOULD YOU LIKE TO MEET THE REAL NADIA?

TARIQ

A **GIRL** might remember a particular incident or a person when she associates the incident or the person with her budding feelings of sexual awakening. I vividly remember that rainy night in my early adolescent years as I sat cross-legged on our living room couch sipping hot tea, eyes glued on the TV screen, watching the queen of seduction Nadia Al Jundi play the role of Zannouba in *The Empress*.

I was mesmerized by Zannouba, by the sharpness of her eyes and the strong tone of her voice. She exuded self-confidence and was unperturbed in the presence of men.

The film tells the story of Zannouba, a maid who falls in love with her employer Ahmad. One day, Ahmad's mom barges into his bedroom and catches him having sex with Zannouba. The mom attacks Zannouba violently, humiliates her, and kicks her out of the house half naked. Zannouba's scandal spreads fast in the neighborhood. Her dishonor brings shame to all her family. Her brother beats her up. Having lost her virginity, the most precious possession a woman in that patriarchal macho society can have, Zannouba is determined to fight the social injustice she's subjected to. She starts thinking of ways to wipe off the shame she has caused herself and her family. She refuses to remain oppressed. Driven by her desire for revenge, she starts planning until she eventually masters her grip on the power tools of that harsh society. She eventually succeeds in reversing her fortune. Once she reaches the top, Zannouba rules the men in her life with no mercy.

She controls them, steers them whichever way she wishes.

She convinces her brothers to start dealing drugs. She employs her seductive skills to ensnare one of the biggest contractors, Mr. Nassar, and marry him. We see her later sitting on the neighborhood throne as an empress, surrounded by men who are ready to do whatever she orders them to do.

Zannouba's previous lover Ahmad, who is a detective, fights her and threatens to annihilate her empire. But she wins in the end. Suppressing her feelings for Ahmed, Zannouba tricks him one night to her lair where she poisons his drink. As he's dying, she kisses him a final kiss and whispers in his ear that she had to avenge herself before he betrayed her again. She cries as he dies in her arms.

I remember the part in *The Empress* which appealed to me the most. It's the scene where Zannouba's husband, after being humiliated by her, asks her for sex. Zannouba treats him with disdain. She sits on her bed, her leg stretched in front of him. She points at her foot and orders him, 'Kiss it'. He obeys without hesitation. Zannouba pushes him away with disgust and kicks him out of the room saying, 'You're not getting any today. You're not spending the night here'.

Seeing Zannouba's husband weak at his wife's feet turned me on. How did she manage to subjugate such an entitled man? I wondered. I didn't understand my feelings that day and didn't know why that particular scene appealed to me. I wasn't aware of the complex emotions and sexual desires I felt as I watched the film, and didn't expect myself fulfilling those desires one day. I didn't really want to be an empress and never dreamt of becoming a drug dealer, nor did I want a life where I treated men and women like that. But during that phase in my life, the idea of controlling and subjugating men sexually started taking shape in my head.

Around the same time, I became attracted to our Egyptian

janitor. I didn't want to have sex with him and wouldn't have done that even if I could, but his image as a tough grownup man serving the women in our building turned me on. I would hide behind our door and watch our neighbor yell at him and order him around. Afraid of losing his job and getting deported back to Egypt, he would beg her to forgive him. Our neighbor had a temper. If she called for him and he didn't hear her or was late in reaching her apartment, she would humiliate and insult him. The injustice of her treatment of the janitor didn't sit well with me. It saddened and angered me. Neither I nor anyone in the building ever stepped up to defend the poor man. Still, there were times when I felt driven by a specific desire, a need to treat him the way our neighbor treated him. I didn't want to humiliate him the way she did, but even at that young age, I knew how to control him. Standing at our door the way our neighbor did, I would call him in the same tone.

'Tamer! Tamer!'

If he arrived late, I would ask him with irritation, 'Where have you been? Why are you late? Mom wants these items from the supermarket,' handing him a grocery list not unlike the one I would write to Firas years later after we got married. I'd read the list out loud to Tamer to make sure he understood what was on it, repeating and emphasizing the most essential things to make sure he wouldn't forget them, before sending him off with, 'Hurry now. Don't be late.'

That was but a small window where society allowed me to fulfill some of my erotic fantasies. Still, I didn't link those fantasies directly to my actual desires. I tried to compartmentalize them and avoided mixing fantasy with reality. I convinced myself that treating Tamer like that was normal. It had no sexual bearings. I was like any other woman in the building treating service people with superiority. I didn't realize it was my way as an adolescent girl of recognizing my sexual identity and living it outside its context.

Back to Nadia Al Jundi's film which I discussed with Tariq during one of our trysts. We were talking about our first sexual-awakening memories. We had a good laugh when I mentioned Nadia Al Jundi's films which he and other men from his generations loved.

'No one could deny it was the sex scenes which attracted men to Nadia's films,' Tariq winked at me. 'But I'm sure the image Nadia presented of the strong woman was the biggest reason those films were successful,' he added, hinting that his sexual fantasies were not peculiarly his but common among a large number of men who resembled him in their willingness to be dominated by women.

'Possibly,' I replied, thinking of my conflicting feelings towards the portrayal of women in Nadia's films. I hated how those powerful women dared to show their strength only after experiencing social injustice. Revenge was usually the main theme and women had to suffer a great deal before they were driven to exercise their power and show their strength, as if a strong woman could not exist naturally the way a man could. As though a woman was required to remain a weakling, let down by society, before she could claw her way out of her old skin and wear the super cape otherwise reserved for men.

I wished we had films depicting strong dominant women who were not subjected to some sort of social injustice. Men's superiority and dominance didn't require justification in Arab culture. Why did women need that?

'Would you like to meet the real Nadia?' I straightened my back and perked my breasts the way Nadia did in her movies. I stood up and looked down at Tariq.

'Yes, I would like that very much, Ma'am,' he answered.

I was wearing a revealing short nightgown and was dreaming of acting out the erotic scene which I had played in my head so many times. I walked toward the bed, sat down, and leaned back on the pillow. Lifting the hem of my nightgown over my thigh as Zannouba did in the movie. I gave Tariq the same look Zannouba gave Nassar, and commanded him in the same tone, 'Kiss it'.

Tariq was quick to sit on the floor by the bed, hold my foot, and kiss it gently.

I wanted him so bad that moment as his fingers circled my ankle and his lips covered the bottom of my foot with gentle kisses and started massaging it. With the same foot, I pushed his head away and said the line from the scene, 'You won't get any today.'

Pretending to rejecting Tariq so forcefully filled me with a raging lust for him. I wanted him with every molecule in my body. Tariq and I couldn't stop laughing as I acted the role. It might have been because the scene itself was awkward and was meant to break so many social taboos. Laughter was our way of reminding ourselves we are just role playing. It was the first time a man kissed my foot. Before Tariq, I had confessed to numerous men I met online that I would be turned on by such an act, but I never actually met any of those men. I was cautious in discovering and understanding my own sexual desires outside the internet world. I wasn't going to try anything while still married to Firas, except with Tariq. He was the only one who attracted me in such a way that surpassed all my dreams and fantasies.

Tariq and I were extremely compatible. We were both aware that our sexual acts, strange and charged as they were, acts which crossed all known social norms, were no more than foreplay. We both enjoyed our roles and bed and cast them off the moment we climaxed. Humiliating Tariq while having sex with him did not affect the way I looked at him and respected him as a man. I wanted to hug him and kiss him because he proved to me that he was ready to do anything I asked from him. I put my arms around his neck and kissed his lips.

'You can get it today and tomorrow and the day after and the day after that,' I whispered in his ear.

I am certain that Tariq remembers that scene as he lies recovering on his bed a week after his discharge from the hospital. I watch him press the remote control, flipping between TV channels. He comes across a rerun of one of Nadia Al Jundi's old movies. I watch him smile. The film has no doubt brought to his mind our memorable sexual encounters. After the impotence he has suffered from since my death, his penis suddenly gets hard. Tariq picks up his phone and Googles "dominant women submissive men". Google offers him a large list of porn movies. Tariq decides on a film based on the star's looks and the title of the film. He spends two hours switching from one film to another, re-watching the scenes which arouse him more and dismissing those which do not match his fantasies. He is horny and wants to have sex but knows he can't have that kind of sex with Ikram. In my absence, he has to find an alternative. He logs on to Facebook, enters his fake screen name, and checks the pages of other dominatrices, until he lands on the page of another Jordanian girl he used to meet for sex before he met me.

He sends her a message: 'I miss you, Ma'am.'

CHAPTER 13

ONCE UPON A TIME, MY QUEEN

TARIQ

O N a quiet Friday evening, I was sipping my coffee in the front garden when a black Peugeot drove up our street and parked at the curb. A man, a woman, and a little toddler girl exited the car. The man carried the girl and crossed the road toward our building, followed by his wife. As they approached the entrance, the man handed the baby to his wife and started talking to the janitor, but the little girl shook off her mother's hand and ran toward our door. Filled with childish curiosity, she stepped into our garden, unaware that I was close by. When she spotted me, she felt embarrassed, unsure of what to do, before turning and running back to her mom. The woman stood by the garden door chastising her daughter and apologizing to me. I got up and approached her, assuring her that her daughter didn't bother me at all and there was no need for her to be punished.

Ikram saw it as a chance to inquire about the building, the neighborhood and the area in general. She was naturally nosey. She asked me about my family, where we came from, and about the name of my husband's family and where *they* came from. She asked me about my husband's job and if I worked and where. When did we get married? Do we have kids? No? She wondered why we still didn't have kids. She encouraged me to have children. Warned me that without children, boredom found its way into a marital relationship fast. Children added life to a relationship and strengthened it, she said.

Ikram gave me no chance to ask her any questions, not that I wanted to. I knew what her husband did. I knew his last name. I knew how many children she had, knew their names and ages. I probably knew more than she did about her husband's needs and fantasies, things he was probably too embarrassed to share with her.

Having finished talking with the janitor, Tariq walked towards us. He greeted me in passing, like two people meeting for the first time. I answered him in the same manner. In truth, I was extremely surprised to see him. I had already ended our relationship after the first meeting in his clinic and stopped answering his calls or replying to his text messages. I didn't expect him to bring his wife and come to view the apartment I had mentioned to him, nor did I think he seriously intended to move his family into our building. I also didn't know if his presence that day was prompted by his view of the suitability of apartment, the location of the building, and the nature of its construction, or if was driven by his desire to be close to me. It was crazy to even consider the second possibility. I couldn't think of a sane man building his future and the future of his family on the sole desire to be close to a woman he met just once. When I asked him about it later, Tariq told me that his visit that day was driven by a mixture of both. He wanted to see me again, but he also needed to find housing for his family. He liked the apartment and the neighborhood and was thrilled to see me. Up until that point, neither one of us had anticipated how things would develop between us. We underestimated the power of feelings between a man and a woman who liked and wanted each other.

I thought about Tariq and Ikram after they left. I tried to find a plausible reason why Tariq would want to cheat on his family. He and Ikram seemed happy to me. I didn't feel there was any tension between them. What I saw was respect and love. They were different from Firas and me. There was harmony in the way they talked to each other. One would think they were newlyweds. They treated each other with enviable tenderness. Ikram had a nice body. She was beautiful, fit, tall with soft rosy skin. She had blue eyes and a sharp shapely nose. Her teeth might have needed braces, but they couldn't be the reason behind Tariq's trysts. She wore a hijab. Her clothes were elegant and classy. Her taste reflected on her clothes as well as her husband's and daughter's. Her appearance gave me an impression of a woman who was successful in taking care of her family, a woman who played her required social role to perfection. But all of that was not enough to make up for the lack Tariq felt in his life. She probably didn't make him feel challenged.

One time, trying to justify why he was attracted to me more than to Ikram, Tariq told me a story. We were playing a role we liked and played often, acting out parts of *Arabian Nights*. But since our relationship was built on the opposite of the traditional cultural roles outlind in *Arabian Nights*, we were not Scheherezade and Shahryar. On the contrary, I was the Sultana and Tariq was the slave who had to serenade and entertain me with stories until daybreak. Since we didn't have the luxury of spending an entire night together, daybreak for us meant the sound of the alarm.

My slave's story that night was so engaging. I, the Sultana, ended up forgiving him and sparing his life. The story surprised me and added a new dimension to the way I understood history and the nature of relationships between men and women.

'My Queen,' he said. 'Do you know that Adam had another wife before Eve?'

My interest was piqued. At first, I thought Tariq was joking or just making up a tale, but he assured me the myth appeared in the Zohar and Jewish folklore.

'This is how the story goes, my Queen. A long time ago, before Eve was created, Adam was married to another woman. It is told that his first wife, whose name was Lilith, which means night in Hebrew, like your name, my Queen, was renowned for her stunning beauty and wit. She was the epitome of perfection. Beautiful Lilith was created from clay like Adam and not from a crooked rib pulled out of Adam's side while he was sleeping, like Eve. The couple were madly in love with each other, living happily in Eden among colorful heavenly birds and all that your heart desires. Everything in Eden, be it animals or birds or reptiles, celebrated the couple's union and love.

'But as we know, my Queen, happiness doesn't last forever, not in this life and not in the hereafter. Lilith viewed herself as equal to Adam and did not allow him to command her. She refused to subjugate her feminine side out of respect or obedience to his masculinity. Lilith wanted to be valued and respected, not to be treated as an inferior. And why not, my Queen? Isn't that her right, she who was made out of clay the way Adam was? That's why arguments and problems erupted between them, threatening their happiness, keeping them awake at night. The biggest of these problems had had to do with the physical relationship between man and woman in bed.'

Tariq was quiet for a second as he kissed my hand and raised his head so I could kiss him on the lips.

'Lilith was convinced,' Tariq continued in a calm voice, 'that her being on top during intercourse asserted her femininity and status as a woman, while Adam staunchly believed that, to affirm his masculinity, he was supposed to be on top. The two lovers differed on how they should make love, both convinced that what took place in bed mirrored their entire relationship.

That's why each one of them refused to give in to the other. They held on to their views and let misery paint their life with its depressing hue.'

Tariq fell silent, a sad look on his face. I patted his head and let him continue.

'Lilith ran away. She left Adam alone, sad, bemoaning his fate and crying his luck. He walked across plains, down valleys and up mountains, swam seas and scanned oceans looking for her without success. When he couldn't find her, he sent three angels out to search for her. He told them to either bring her back or kill her. But Lilith refused to come back. When Adam gave up on her return and was consumed by sadness, God created Eve to keep him company.

'Myth also has it that Adam never forgot Lilith,' Tariq continued. 'He never loved Eve the way he loved Lilith. What I find interesting about this myth is how the story unfolds and follows Lilith who apparently falls in love with the devil and marries him to sends a message to Adam. As a punishment, Lilith is cursed for eternity and doomed to see one hundred of her children killed every day. That's why she decides to take revenge on the children of Adam and Eve. Different myths depict her as the Angel of Death, or an owl which appears at night and targets the offspring of Adam and Eve. She appears through history as an evil spirit recognized by many pregnant women today, haunting their dreams, trying to snatch their children and kill them before they are born or in the crib. Some myths even say Lilith herself is the snake which appeared to Adam and Even in Eden and seduced them to eat the forbidden fruit.'

It wasn't enough for Tariq to tell me the story. He pointed out how the legend of Lilith was absent from our Arab culture despite having a strong presence among feminist groups in the West.

'Burying the story, even if it was just a myth, indicates the prevalence of chauvinistic masculine thinking in our societies,' he said. 'Lilith's fall and the emergence of monotheistic religions in their current patriarchal form are ultimately linked with the biased demotion of women and their subjugation to men throughout history.'

Tariq was right in how he saw women marginalized in our societies, made to look like the devil and attacked like Lilith was attacked. A woman was hated and viewed as a menace if she rebelled against the man. Her act was a considered a threat to family stability and society in general. If she refused to adhere to man's control and power, a woman was viewed as disposable. She deserved to be killed, to be called names, to become a cautionary tale for other women. I was aware of that. It was evident in my rebellion against Firas and the norms of the society I grew up in, a society which equated femininity to weakness and powerlessness. I was a woman who acknowledged and embraced her sexual needs. I refused to settle for less.

'Chauvinistic thinking does not oppress women only, but men too,' Tariq added after a short pause. 'It oppresses men who, like me, admire strong independent women and are not shamed of their sexual preferences. It tries to shame us, doubts our manhood, and taints the way society views us.'

There are so many men like Tariq who fall between the anvil of chauvinistic culture which gives them the right to control and lead and the hammer of their natural preference to be submissive. Ikram was to Tariq what Eve was to Adam – a woman he could control. I was Lilith, the seductress he could not get and could not subjugate.

'A man who is submissive sexually is rejected the way a woman who is dominant sexually is rejected, my Queen,' Tariq said as the alarm went off signaling that our time together had come to an end.

CHAPTER 14

HE HAS TO BE EXECUTED PUBLICLY AT THE HASHEMITE PLAZA

FIRAS

FIRAS was not only unlucky, but extremely unfortunate during that phase of his life. It might have been bad karma, or destiny's way of making him pay for the miserable days I lived with him. The stars might have been misaligned. Or it might have been his consistently negative personality which saw the glass half full even if it was filled to the brim with distilled water. Whichever one it is, bad luck pursued him, turning his life, which he already viewed as unbearable, into a living hell.

If I possessed the power to change the course of events, or had the means to influence fate, I would have written the story differently. I would have changed its course and would have adopted a more lenient tone toward Firas. Even though I had negative, unhealthy feelings toward him which at times felt like pure hatred, I never really wished that ending upon him. Our unhappy marriage and the year he spent without a job were enough punishment for him. But marital infidelity, be it secret or known, is something only horrible people deserve. Fate alone was not to be blamed for those three mishaps in Firas's life. Firas's immaturity and reckless behavior were largely to blame. He was responsible for the failure of our marriage and responsible for refusing to work because he was stubborn. His rude, crude nature played a major part in pushing me away from him and throwing me in the arms of another man. But arriving late to the house the day I died could only be interpreted as bad luck. From that point on, Firas's fate was sealed. His lack of interaction with the detectives, as well as his sour relationship with my family and me, were key in how fast the accusation stuck to him. But Firas was innocent of murder and didn't deserve the infamy he and his family were subjected to. Amman's harsh society was ready to judge others more brutally than the law would have judged them. Murder was unforgivable, especially when the victim was a beautiful young woman who happened to be the only child of an influential, well-respected family.

Firas's friendships suddenly evaporated. His best friends turned against him. No one stood by him and no one wanted to have anything to do with him and his family. Everyone, even their closest friends, shunned them. Firas refused to confess to a crime he didn't commit. He remained unshakable in face of psychological and physical abuse he was subjected to while being interrogated. But the story which spread twisted the truth completely. It exaggerated the events which led to my death and made Firas appear to have confessed to the crime.

Once the shock of my death wore off, even Rawan, our dear friend who was privy to the nature of our relationship and our problems, started talking negatively about Firas to her friends, describing him as a psychopathic murderer. She would wipe her tears and try to control herself as she talked, the words suffocating her.

'Animal!' she'd proclaim, shaking her head and repeating the word with emphasis. 'Animal! I still can't believe what happened. I'm still in shock.'

Then, she would add with a sigh, 'I had a feeling all along that he was unstable. There was something wrong with him. But I never imagined he would do that! Can you imagine he went with her dad looking for her the night he killed her?' She would be silent for a few seconds before adding, 'Sick! He is a sick sociopath.' With that, she would reflect quietly, recalling me talking to her about Firas, telling her he was nuts. That was how I described him toward the end when he became uncontrollable and his actions were extremely erratic. Rawan would get lost in her thoughts, probably remembering my voice as I admitted to her how unhappy I was in my marriage, confessing to her that I wanted to divorce Firas. She might recall how warned my against that, how she reasoned with me and asked me to wait, how she encouraged me to try to work on my marriage and try to fix it.

Sobbing, she would pick her cell phone to look through her photo album before finding a photo of Firas and me. A photo from our wedding, hugging, looking so much in love and harmony. Another photo of us smiling among friends in the first days of our marriage. In the photo, I'm sitting next to Firas, my head on his shoulder, his arm around my waist, his lips planting a kiss on my forehead. He used to show his love at that time by staying close to me when we went out, his eyes, like laser beams, scanning the men around us, marking his territory. He did that either to protect me or to show that as his wife, I belonged to him and him alone.

Flipping through the photos, Rawan would come across a screenshot of an article which appeared in an online paper: "HUSBAND TORTURES WIFE TO DEATH IN SWEIFIEH", followed by another article with the headline: "HUSBAND KILLS WIFE AND THROWS HER BODY IN DUMPSTER ON AIRPORT ROAD." She would pass her phone to one of her friends to show him the photos and he would pass it to another. They would shake their heads in disbelief, appalled by the horrible crime. They would concur that Firas had received the right sentence and should be executed. They would proclaim death itself not enough for a criminal like him. According to them, Firas deserved to be tortured first before he was executed.

'He has to be executed publicly in Hashemite Plaza,' Rawan would say.

As usual, no one would contradict her. Everyone would nod in agreement.

Even my mom agreed with Rawan. She collected newspaper clips mentioning me, saved them in a box labeled with my name and containing photos of me since birth. She prayed to God every day asking Him to make Firas's mom taste the bitterness she herself had tasted. She would sit on the kitchen chair for hours consumed by sorrows, telling my dad and everyone who cared to listen how she wished Firas could be hanged publicly in the plaza for all to see. She told my dad she daydreamed about carrying out the death sentence herself. But she didn't just imagine herself hanging Firas. She dreamt about attacking him brutally, scratching his face with her nails and tightening her fingers around his neck, squeezing hard and not letting go until he stopped breathing.

She refused the blood money Firas's family offered. She threatened to leave my dad if he relinquished his rights and accepted the money. She screamed at him, 'Did you lose your mind? Are you crazy? Do you want your daughter's rights wasted and trampled on? That animal should be executed or left to rot in jail for the rest of his life.'

The only one who believed in Firas's innocence was his mom, who knew her son and loved him more than anyone else. She never tired of calling my mom. She called every day, stayed on the line hoping she would pick up. When she gave up on my mom, she called my dad, sobbing when she heard his voice. She begged him, 'Please listen to me, Abu Laila. I swear to God Firas is innocent. He didn't kill her. I swear to God he's innocent.'

She begged him to drop the charges, but he refused. His

answers were curt. He told her to leave it to the courts to take their course and not to call him again. She asked if she could talk to my mom, hoping my mom would be kinder to her and her son. But my mom raised her finger in my dad's face, warning him not to hand her the receiver.

'Laila's mom isn't feeling well and can't talk,' my dad said before hanging up.

My mom wasn't feeling well for real. She couldn't bear the idea of talking to Firas's mom. Nothing could ease her pain, not even the death sentence which would be handed down to Firas in a few days. The sentence didn't make her feel better because it didn't bring me back to her. She even doubted that the sentence would be carried out because the death penalty was put on hold in Jordan eight years before.

Thanks to the Arab Spring, my mother's hope was revived. Driven by a political decision to rehabilitate the country's image after the instability of the Arab Spring and a sharp spike in crime, the Jordanian government reinstated some draconian measures. One of them was the resumption of the death penalty. It was to be carried out on eleven individuals sentenced to death for crimes they had committed.

As I said, Firas was unfortunate and fate was determined to side against him until his last breath. He was not among the eleven criminals executed that day, but that didn't mean he was not going to be executed in the few coming days.

At dawn one day, he was led out of his cell to pay the price for a crime he didn't commit.

CHAPTER 15

I FELT I WAS BECOMING HER

TARIQ

I DON'T think Tariq was missing Mona when he messaged her. He just needed an outlet to escape the emotional pressure tightening its grip on him. He was longing for a woman to pull him out of reality, someone who could help him forget me. A woman who would give him some of what he missed now that I was gone.

I knew that Tariq met Mona in the past for sex. Pure emotionless sex, void of the feelings he and I shared. He was not attracted to Mona physically or taken by her wit. He told me that he avoided spending time talking to her outside the context of sex.

Tariq had met Mona twice in the past when the need to have sex was so strong and she was the only one available. Each time Tariq left her place, he decided not to see her again. Almost everything about her, from her scrawny body, to her perfume and her breath, repulsed him. Mona was a chain smoker. The cigarette might have been a symbol of power for her, a challenge to a society which looked down on women who smoked. Or she might have seen cigarettes the way a teenager boy viewed them - a sign of his maturity or a symbol of his manhood. Approaching forty, Mona didn't need a cigarette to signal her maturity nor did she need it to signify masculinity. She might have seen the cigarette as an extension of her femininity, an accessory adorning her freedom and confirming her independence as a woman in charge of making her own decisions. She liked to hold a cigarette between her fingers as she looked down with superiority on a submissive man kneeling at her feet. She would pull on her cigarette, bring her face closer to his, and blow out smoke in his eyes, laughing at his reaction. Or she would tap her cigarette and let the ash fall on his face.

Like me, Mona had been trapped in a marriage lacking sexual compatibility, with a husband who was as bad as Firas. In fact, he was probably worse than Firas. He was violent, brutal, and rude to her. She got married at a young age and didn't have a job, so she wasn't financially independent. She came from a conservative poor family. That's why she couldn't stand up to her husband or express her needs and desires to him. She accepted her fate and put up with her husband for years. At the beginning of her marriage, she looked at what turned her on sexually as shameful. But with time, she gained enough strength to rebel, and she became more aware of her needs. She found ways to fulfill them and satisfy herself.

She might have been weaker than me when it came to her fear of a face-to-face encounter with her husband and her wish to avoid violence and arguments. But she was stronger than me in holding to her principles. It's possible that she just didn't meet the man who could steal her heart and make her throw her principles to the wind, as I did when I met Tariq. She didn't cheat on her husband, regardless of how repulsed she was by him. She attempted to express her needs to him, but he didn't understand her, just as I had tried to express my needs to Firas. She waited until she found a job and became financially independent before she had the courage to ask for a divorce. When he refused, she divorced him and kicked him out of the apartment she paid for with her salary.

Mona gained her freedom and supported her only child. She swore off marriage, but she didn't deny herself the pleasure of fulfilling her physical needs. She learned how to arrange sexual rendezvous whenever it pleased her. She looked for men who were driven by a desire to satisfy women sexually.

She lured them to her room and ordered them around. Ironically, Mona's sexual satisfaction didn't necessarily require a consummation of the sexual act. In other words, sex for her didn't require a man's penis penetrating her vagina. That's why she didn't consider her trysts with men as to be at opposite ends with her principles.

When Tariq knocks on Mona's door, he is well aware of her past and proclivities and is ready to fulfill the role required from him. I hear his knock and I feel my heart being squeezed. It beats anew as though life has started coursing through it. These are the knocks my ears were accustomed to in life, my heart ready to dance whenever Tariq came to see me.

I feel myself blend into Mona when she opens the door for him. She and I both exist in the moment. Our souls subconsciously fight for control. I try to push her body to get closer to Tariq's. She has feelings for him. I sense that. It's as if she has absorbed in the scent of my love for him. But she is quick to check herself and stem that strange feeling. She looks at him with disdain and treats him with superiority.

'Why are you late?' she asks him in a harsh tone.

'I'm sorry, Ma'am' he answers meekly, even though he has arrived on time.

He shows her the same submissiveness he has shown me. The same acquiescence which increases my longing to the point that I almost push Mona against her will to get closer to him and hug him. But, despite my success in stirring her feelings, I can't physically move her. She is the kind of woman who can control her body, regardless of the strength of her passion. She remains poised and waves him inside.

'Come on in.'

Tariq follows her quietly. She walks in front of him until they reach the room she has reserved and prepared for such meetings. She orders him to go in.

'Take off your clothes and kneel on the floor. When I come back, I want to find you waiting for me with your hands behind your back. Understood?'

Tariq nods yes. Mona leaves us. I float in the room around him. I try to communicate with him, but I fail. Still, I sense him experience a feeling of peace and tranquility, the same serenity he has only felt with me.

Mona comes back in fifteen minutes. She's wearing army fatigues and carrying handcuffs. Her costume takes me off guard. I have never been that creative.

I am quick to blend with her and absorb her emotions. She and I approach Tariq quietly. He doesn't raise his head. We both bend down and handcuff him. We make sure the handcuffs are secure around his wrists. Make sure he can't move. We bring a kerchief and blindfold him. Mona lights a cigarette and takes a deep pull. I like her composure and self-confidence. I admire the way she controls the submissive man at her feet.

The curtains are drawn and the only light in the room comes from the candles Mona has lit around the corners. She approaches one of these corners and lifts up a candle. She walks toward Tariq with the candle in her hand and lifts his chin. She holds the candle above him and quietly tilts it, letting the melted wax drip on his chest. Tariq screams in pain and my soul cries for him. Mona laughs and brings the candle closer so the sting of its hot wax burns him more acutely. I realize how different she is from me. She isn't only turned on by controlling men, but also by inflicting physical pain on them. Tariq doesn't object to physical pain during sex if his partner enjoys it. But his visit to Mona today is not driven by a desire to satisfy her only. He wants to feel pain in hope that the pain will overpower the agony consuming him since my death. Or it might be something inside him telling him he deserves to suffer physically to atone for his inability to confess the truth and save Firas from the gallows.

I used to hit him, but not as a punishment. I hit him to push him to make the right decision. Still, I never hurt him the way Mona is hurting him. Whether he likes it or not, I can't stand still without interfering when I see him suffering in front of me. But despite my seeming powerlessness to affect the material world, my will to protect Tariq leads me to find an in-between channel linking our two worlds. I blow at the candle Mona is holding in her hand before more wax drips on Tariq's body. Mona doesn't like that. She quickly brings the tip of the candle to another lit candle in the corner of the room to light it, but the flame of second candle dies too. When she reaches for the third one, it too loses its flame. Same with the fourth and fifth candles, until darkness engulfs the room.

Mona throws the candle to the side and walks toward Tariq in the darkness. Suddenly, her spirit vanishes, leaving her body behind for me to connect with Tariq. He no longer feels her presence. Instead, he senses me in her body and feels me get closer to him. I hug his head. Tariq lets the flood of emotions filling the room engulf him. Despite the chains restraining his movement, he opens his mouth and moves it voraciously over Moan's body. My body.

I am quick to take off the army pants Mona is wearing. I step closer to Tariq. I can feel his kisses on the way I've always felt them. I hold his head and pull him toward me and let him lick me.

I am about to climax and feel him climaxing with me.

The strength of our passion and the enormity of our longing bind our bodies in ecstasy. It takes over us at the same moment. Our bodies tremble in a way we never felt before.

Internal darkness pervades after that and my soul

disconnects and floats outside the room.

Mona comes to, the inexplainable shock of what just happened, a glazed look in her eyes.

CHAPTER 16

EASY, EASY MA'AM

TARIQ

TARIQ closes his clinic and stays inside it the day after he sees Mona. He asks his assistant to cancel all his appointments. He sits behind his desk crying. He is no longer able to concentrate on his patients and feels he can't go about his daily life in a normal way.

I think that seeing Mona the night before has been hard on him because it reignited the strength of his feelings for me and made him more aware of how much he missed me. He appears sorry for what he did with her, as if having sex with Mona has made him unfaithful to me. I know that the intensity of his lovemaking that night has been possible because I was there. But he is aware that he made love to Mona and not to me. That saddens him.

In spite of Tariq's powerful emotions, he suspects that they stem from a connection to my soul, as opposed to a connection with Mona's body which continues to repel him. But the way she climaxed as she reached to squeeze his left earlobe was an intimate touch I had every time I climaxed, a reflection of the surging emotions he stirred inside me. But try as he can, he still can't explain the darkness which engulfed the room that night and how he lost consciousness for a few seconds afterwards.

After his experience with Mona, Tariq seems sad. He moves slowly and laboriously, as if he's shackled by misery, or plunged into darkness. He finds himself a prisoner to the memory of another scene between us. He is terrified by the memory. His fear is not limited to the way he has dealt with my body after I died. It's driven by a need to resist a feeling of guilt, an admission of being directly responsible for my death.

Tariq was my doctor and my lover. He was aware of my heart condition. Had he thought rationally about it, he would have refused to succumb to his desire to be completely submissive to me. He would have objected to having me tie him up because that rendered him powerless to act quickly and save me from death in case my heart suddenly stopped. But Tariq either ignored the possibility because he wanted to try something new with me. Or he might have never expected my heart to stop suddenly the way it did.

He sounded reluctant as he nodded in agreement when I suggested the idea. 'Your wish is my command, Ma'am,' he said in his usual way of agreeing to everything I asked from him. I wasn't particularly keen on the idea of a dominatrix strapping on a dildo and penetrating a submissive man. I had conflicting feelings when I first saw that in a porn film. On one hand, I refused the prevalent way of thinking that a man had the right to lead the sexual act just because he had a penis. I knew that I didn't have to play the role of the man or to borrow any of his parts to reassert my sexual dominance over him. My femininity was perfect just as my body was beautiful. It was what defined me as a woman and gave me the feeling of dominance. It was what made men weak in front of me.

On the other hand, I wasn't blind to the prevalent belief that finds it insulting for men to accept that sexual position. The public views a man in that position as weak because he has accepted the receiving role meant for a woman. How can he allow a woman to play the role of a man and deprive him of his masculinity?

I didn't intend to play the role of a man, but the idea of humiliating Tariq like that turned me on. I saw a difference between man being submissive sexually and submissive socially. Sexual submissiveness did not necessarily point to weakness; on the contrary, it was a sign of courage only a few men possessed. By giving up their own willpower to please their partners in bed, those men showed strength of character.

Tariq's strong personality intensified my desire for him. His submissiveness to me fueled my willpower and satisfied my ego. I might have seen in his submissiveness a form of love. Infinite unchained love. Love which drove a man to give in to what his beloved wanted even if it meant giving up his role and identity and social standing. But Tariq's submissiveness to me, be it weakness or strength, love or desire, did not necessitate penetrating him with a dildo. Our sex usually ended with me commanding him to please me. That usually meant him penetrating me vaginally. That act in itself did not make me feel subjugated to him but emphasized his submissiveness to me and my control over him. I was the one leading the sexual act. I was the one commanding him to lie on his back so I could mount him and ride him and be control of the rhythm of our sex from start to finish. There were times when I decided to mount him after I tied his hands behind his back to limit his movement and restrict his ability to resist. In short, the idea of penetrating him with a dildo while he was tied up and unable to move turned me on in a strange way, probably because acting that role reasserted my power over his own body and my ability to steer it in any direction I chose.

That day, despite not having slept well, I could not waste the chance of having Firas outside the house. I was so nervous. My emotions were boiling. I felt powerless toward my relationship with Firas and more powerless toward my relationship to Tariq, especially after I asked Firas for a divorce numerous times and then changed my mind. Under pressure from Firas, his family, and our common friends, I tried to save our marriage, A part of me might have unconsciously held on to Firas or to my life with him. Or I maybe I was afraid of change and just got used to the way things were between us.

Like me, Tariq was powerless when it came to leaving Ikarm. She was smart. She didn't allow lack of sexual compatibility to affect other parts of their relationship. She probably failed to recognize Tariq's peculiar needs and therefore never actually rejected them, but never tried to fulfill them. Tariq didn't have the courage to come forward and express to her what he wanted. He tried in the past to relax his body and let her lead the sexual act, but she didn't understand him. Instead, she would put her head on his chest, thinking he was resting before resuming what he had started. Being the one in control probably didn't suit Ikram. Maybe that was why she always waited for him to resume his role as the leader of the sex act, the way she liked it.

Tariq confided in me that he didn't have a strong desire to have sex with his wife, but he didn't mind being intimate with her every now and then. On the other hand, Ikram never complained and never pressured him or made him feel he was lacking in his duties. She always treated him as the man of the house. In return, she was proud of herself as a good housewife, carrying out all her duties to perfection without asking for his help. Their house and their clothes were always clean and tidy. Her cooking was delicious. She knew exactly what he liked to eat and made sure to cook it for him. She took care the children, fed them and disciplined them and reviewed their schoolwork with them. She gave him no reason to ask for a divorce. But Tariq and I were both aware that what we had between us could not last in secret. We knew we couldn't end our relationship. We felt so strongly about each other and couldn't escape or ignore our feelings. There was simply no way of going back.

We found ourselves in a hard place, an impossible situation that couldn't go on and had no solution. Despite Tariq's strong feelings for his family, despite how hard it would be for him to walk out on them, despite me telling him repeatedly that I was not the kind of woman who would take him away from his kids, despite me assuring him that leaving Firas did not mean he would have to leave Ikram, he surprised me last Sunday at his clinic by telling me he was going to divorce her after I left Firas. He broke then news to me as he put the stethoscope on my chest to check for signs of heart murmur. My heartbeats were irregular, and my condition had worsened under the mental pressure I was going through. I felt exhausted all the time and was prone to bouts of shortness of breath. I was feeling nauseous when I went to his clinic and asked him to check me.

My heartbeats might have warned him that I would not last for long. Time was ready to betray us and deprive us of our happy moments. Tariq put the stethoscope aside and asked me to lie down on the examination table. He climbed up and lay next to me. He put his arm around my head and rested it on his shoulder. He held my hand and kissed my palm, swept my hair behind my ear and whispered, 'Don't worry, Ma'am. Everything will happen the way we want it.'

I smiled and said nothing because I thought it was more of a wish than a fact. I let my head rest on his shoulder dreamily and let the music of his whispers serenade my ears. He continued his vision of a future which was a mixture of fantasy and reality. 'You'll leave Firas and I'll leave Ikram.' He kissed me on the cheek and added, 'And then we'll get married, Ma'am.'

'And we'll live happily ever after.' He kissed my shoulder.

'And you will be my Queen, all day and all night.' He kissed my forehead.

My head was resting on his chest and my eyes gazing at the ceiling, living his dream. But I was realistic. I didn't want our madness to push us to commit social suicide. Getting married soon after our divorce would raise questions and create a scandal. Because he was my neighbor and a father of three children, I would bear the brunt of the stigma and give Firas ammunition to fight me and distort my image in front of everyone.

'Tariq, it's too early for this talk,' I said, busting his dream. 'First of all, ending my relationship with Firas will take time. Second of all, I most certainly will not marry again before a year has passed after my divorce. And thirdly, you have young kids and you can't walk out on them at that age.'

I felt winded so I stopped talking and put my hand on my chest, trying to catch my breath.

Tariq put his hand over mine and pressed it. He kissed my forehead again and whispered, 'Don't worry and just rest, Ma'am. There's a time for everything. We won't decide right now. Just think about it. All I want to say is that I'm ready to do anything for you. Anything to make you feel better.'

But what he said didn't make me feel better. Since that day, I started imagining my life with him and the happiness I would have after marrying him. I wondered if the dream would one day become a reality. Would I ever sleep next to him and wake up in the morning to his voice and laughter? Brag to everyone about him, about his success and what he had achieved in life? Boast about his love for me and readiness to serve me and submit to me? We were going to have the world. We were going to be the perfect couple, equal in rights and duties and compatible in our sexual life. Love would unite us, and passion would fill our hearts.

I couldn't wait to hug him when he knocked at my door like a thief that doomed day. He was carrying a bag filled with the items we had agreed on. I was feeling tired that morning, but seeing Tariq filled me with energy. I snatched the bag from him, threw it aside, and hugged him. I had missed him much more than I missed having sex with him. I wanted to have him with me because that feeling of instability and uncertainty wore me out. Or it might have been that morning's strange alarming premonition, a nagging feeling that my end was near. The same feeling Tariq probably had when he told me he was ready to marry me. I wanted to rest my head on his shoulder. I wanted to forget all my problems and pain. I missed the softness of his shirt and was dying to hold him. I held his hand and led him to the couch. He lay down and I slept on his chest. I kissed him as if for the last time.

After I had a dose of his tenderness, I started kissing his lips. I kissed him over and over and over again until my desire for him was too strong. I sat in his lap. I was completely aroused. I wanted to bounce on him. I put my palm on his forehead and pushed his head backward. I slapped him and ordered him to open his mouth. When he did, I spat in it and slapped him one more time as I asked, 'Who is your mistress?'

'You are,' he replied.

Having a tight grip on him turned me on insanely. I held his head to my chest and whispered in his ear, 'Carry me to the bedroom.'

He picked me up easily and headed to the bedroom where he lowered me on the bed like a queen, the way I had taught him. He kissed my hands and legs and feet. But I didn't want to continue the game like that. My plan for our date was more risqué. I got up and indicated to him to bring the bag he brought with him from the living room. I snatched it from him when he did and spread its contents on the bed and ordered him to take off his clothes.

I blindfolded him using the blindfold he had brought from Paris, and ordered him to lie on his stomach and not move. I took out the ropes from the bag. They were four ropes with the correct length I had asked him to buy. Each one was long enough to tie each limb to the closest bedpost.

I got ready for my role. I tightened the knots around his wrists and ankles, restricting his movement. When I was done, I strapped on the dildo. I lathered lubricant on his rectum and started pushing the dildo inside him. I felt him tense. He squeezed his muscles as if he was afraid. For a second, my wedding night flashed in front of me and I remembered feeling the same thing then. I wasn't afraid on my wedding night, but I was apprehensive of the pain I expected to accompany sex. I was still a virgin then, just like Tariq was when I penetrated him. On my wedding night, I asked Firas to go slow, which he did. Like him, I took it easy with Tariq. I didn't want to hurt him. He was asking me not to rush.

'Easy, Ma'am. Easy. Easy. Take it slow, Ma'am. Slow. Slow.'

I remembered the pain I felt the first time I had sex with Firas, but the feeling of ecstasy helped me endure the pain. I had no idea if Tariq would feel the same level of pain or if he would even experience ecstasy when I entered him. I kissed his shoulder and his neck. I felt his muscles relax a little after he realized the dildo was already inside him. The pain he felt was bearable. I soon discovered that the friction created by the dildo against my cervix filled me with a wonderful feeling.

After we conquered our initial fear, I wanted to move the dildo more, pushing it in and out of Tariq. I was surprised to hear Tariq moan. He seemed to be enjoying what was happening, despite the pain on his face. As harmony between our movements grew and our ecstasy intensified, I pushed harder and harder. I was finding it hard to breathe. I tried to control my climax, but my desire was so strong. It drove me to continue what I was doing with abandon, until I felt my body tremble.

I felt waves of ecstasy course through my body, each

stronger than the one before it. With each wave, I found it harder to catch my breath, until I felt my body go limp and my forehead hit the back on Tariq's head, making a dull thud. I heard Tariq scream in pain. Limp, I fell on the sharp edge of the scissors I had left on the bed after cutting the ropes. The scissors left a small cut on my side. I didn't feel any pain when my head hit Tariq's, nor did I feel any pain when the sharp point of the scissors cut my side. My soul had already left my body and floated upward like a helium balloon. It rested against the ceiling. I started laughing. I thought that someone was playing a trick on me. I thought that Tariq had made me smell some hallucinogenic drug which caused me to lose my inhibitions and laugh hysterically.

I laughed even more as I saw fear contort Tariq's face. He was trying to understand what happened to me. I laughed again when he called me tenderly at first: 'Ma'am?' And laughed harder when his tone changed and became more persistent. 'Laila? *Laila?*' I almost fell from the ceiling laughing as I saw him tremble uncontrollably, trying to free himself from the ropes around his limbs.

I was laughing as he tried to free himself from the bondage to save me. I was unaware of the extent of catastrophe which just took place. When he finally managed to free himself, he held my wrist to find out if I had a pulse. When the morbid truth of finding no pulse hit him, he hurriedly performed CPR to revive me. He pressed on my chest. He took a deep breath and breathed it out into my mouth, but I didn't respond. I watched him from above, enjoying his anguish and concern for my wellbeing. He knew he was pressed for time and had to act quickly if he wanted to save me. He performed compressions on my chest again, but my rib cage could not take the pressure. One of my ribs broke under his hands.

I yelled at him: 'Are you stupid?' 'Are you a jackass?' 'Shame on you, man.' 'Has fear blinded you to this extent?'

I stopped reproaching him when I saw him collapse on the floor next to my corpse. It might have been fatigue or fear or probably sadness or regret. He fell on top of me and started sobbing.

'Are you crying? A big man like you cries?' I mocked him.

After a few minutes, he realized the unenviable situation he was in. No one would believe the kind of kinky sex we had. Being unfaithful to our spouses in my own house was enough to incriminate both of us. Finding me dead with a bruise on my head, a cut on my side, and a broken rib would be enough to incriminate him. He would be accused of rape and of mutilating the body of the victim. He deduced that even if he could overcome the scandal, even if he called the ambulance which could no longer save me, he would not be able to convince the police or anyone else of his innocence.

He had to act fast. And as we know, he acted without thinking.

CHAPTER 17

I HAD TO WAIT FOR HIM

FIRAS

AT dawn on a Friday, Firas is taken from his miserable prison cell to the office of the prison warden in Jwaideh Reform and Rehabilitation Center. Powerless, he drags his feet. He is powerless. All the misery of the world is on his bowed head.

He walks into a room full of scowling serious faces. He realizes he has lost the fight. He has never felt like this in his entire life. The sense of condemnation in the room is palpable. In front of him, in the center, sits the prison warden, looking calm and poised. His composure is at odds with the present moment. On the right of the warden, sitting on old worn-out leather seats, are Amman's Deputy Prosecutor and District Attorney, flanked by their assistants. On the other side, the sheikh and the coroner.

The handcuffs are removed from Firas's hands and feet. He is handed a paper on which is written his death sentence and the day it will be carried out. Firas opens his eyes incredulously as he reads the sentence, unable to comprehend what's happening. He can't believe how fast things have moved since the day I died. He can't accept how everything has turned against him. He seems unable to conceive of the fact that a death sentence is issued against him. Deep inside, he has clung to a sense of final justice, some sort of unshakable faith that fate will not fail an innocent man and make him pay for a crime he didn't commit. His mind can't process that fate has let him down. He cannot accept that his death sentence, as stated on the paper in his hand, is going to be carried out in an hour. He doesn't realize that life doesn't necessarily sand on the side of justice, and reality can be more brutal than the worst evil created by the most sadistic imagination. He has forgotten that injustice is nothing but life's disguised way of creating a balance. He is not the only one dealt an unfair blow in this story. I lost my life before him. On top of that, I am stuck between two worlds, unable to go back and incapable of leaving. I can't leave Tariq grappling with his longing to me and can't ignore the injustice Firas is facing. I am shackled to invisible cuffs similar to the ones Firas had a few seconds ago and to the ropes which restrained Tariq the day I died.

The three of us stand helpless in front of death, each one of us seeing it from a different angle. Each one of us follows the development of his story as it intertwines with the two other stories. Tariq is not in a better place than the two of us. He is still in the grip of a bleak emotional struggle. He will not forget what happened for years.

I have no intention of going easy on Tariq. My constant presence doesn't help soothe his nerves or assuage his conscience. I haunt his dreams almost daily, appearing at a distance with my back to him, standing silently and not responding to him when he calls my name and attempts to follow me. In his dreams, I either don't hear him or I ignore him. My body sways and slides away every time he approaches me and tries to touch my dress. The same dream is repeated the next night. Tariq screams and begs me, 'Don't get mad at me, Ma'am. Don't be upset with me, love,' right before he falls to the ground, exhausted, sweating profusely. Only then do I turn my face toward him. My image becomes focused, bigger, my head as big as the full moon in the sky behind me. My eyebrows knitted and my eyes sparkle with anger. My voice is cold, dry, and harsh as death itself.

'Firas is innocent,' I say to Tariq every night. And every night, he begs me to forgive him. He promises to fix everything. He says he can't continue living if I'm angry at him. He promises to go to the police to confess and face the consequences.

The dream always ends there, but not tonight. Tonight, the dream continues to the end.

Tonight, I don't feel sorry for him and don't hear his imploring pleas. I point at two men standing to my left and right, wearing police uniform. I mime to them to arrest Tariq and hang him on a rope which suddenly appears tied on the branch of a huge apple tree. Tariq screams, terrified, as the rope transforms to a boa constrictor wrapping around his neck and restricting his breath. He kicks and fights and tries to breathe. He wakes up. Ikram rushes to bring him a glass of water to calm him down. My shadow floats around the room. Tariq drinks the water and tries to go back to sleep. Ikram lies next to him as my shadow hovers around him. He feels me approach him in a way he has never felt before, so he becomes worried and loses sleep completely. He hears the dawn prayers from the nearby mosque and his heart flutters. The surreal tone of the adhan shakes him to the core. He opens his eyes and asks for forgiveness. For the first time since my death, my entire body materializes in front of him.

Tariq leaves his bed and goes to check on his children. At first, he goes into Qais's room and approaches his bed. He finds his son fast asleep, his pajama top receding, exposing his belly; his bedcover has slipped to the floor. Tariq touches the hem of the pajama top and pulls it down to cover his son's tummy. He picks up the comforter and tucks it gently around Qais as if he's trying to protect his son from what the future has in store for him. He kisses Qais's forehead and leaves. He walks to Salam and Mira's room. He approaches each one and checks to see if she's sleeping peacefully. He kisses his daughters on their foreheads and leaves.

Tariq goes back to his room and gets dressed. Ikram wakes up and he tells her he is going to the Fajr prayer. Ikram is surprised because this is so unlike him, but she says nothing. Tariq heads to his car without thinking, determined to free himself from the nightmare which has taken over his life. When he approaches his car, I find myself suddenly worried about him. What if goes to the police to tell them what happened but the police don't believe? What if they accuse him of killing me? What if I save Firas from the gallows only to have Tariq hang instead and pay the price of a crime he himself has not committed?

Will the police be more careful this time? Or will they only pay lip service to investigating, deciding instead to create a scenario easier to believe than Tariq's preposterous story? Would the judge be more lenient? Or would he hand Tariq a harsh sentence?

I can't think and I can't find a way out except by gathering all my energy and focusing it on the front tire of Tariq's car. My concentrated will pierces the thick rubber like a sharp needle. The air seeps out of it the way life seeps out of a corpse. Tariq stands aghast, unable to believe what's happening in front of him. He doesn't attribute what he sees to any supernatural powers and doesn't think I have anything to do with it, but having a flat tire hinders and delays him. Before he gets the spare out of the trunk, he decides to head to the mosque and pray Fajr.

Tariq washes up at the sink in the mosque backyard. He leaves his shoes by the entrance and enters the almost empty hall. He raises his arms to the sky, imploring God to be merciful toward him. He kneels to the ground and asks his creator to guide him to do the right thing. When he's done with his prayers, Tariq gets up to fetch his shoes. I see this as an opportunity to delay him again. I want to hide the shoes from him, but I don't have the power to move physical things. I might be able to make another man wear Tariq's shoes by mistake, but there is no one close by, so instead, I try to distract Tariq. I succeed momentarily when he fails to see the shoes in front of him. He huffs angrily, thinking that someone might have stolen them. He looks again in the same spot and finds them there. He puts his shoes on and heads to his car, but when he reaches it, he changes his mind. He considers the flat tire a sign from God. He heads back to his house, thanking God.

At the same time, in the cramped office of the prison warden, Firas is losing his mind. He balls the paper stating his death sentence in his fist and throws it at the warden, screaming and cursing. He clenches his fist and aims it at the warden's nose. The warden swiftly tilts his head backward, narrowly avoiding the punch. Firas bounces on the warden as if he intends to kill him, but the other men in the room quickly pin Firas to the floor. The detective brings a tranquilizer and injects it into Firas's arm. Firas calms down as the medicine travels through his veins. The idea of leaving the world, innocent or guilty, no longer frightens him. I feel him wither and see his body collapse. He is slowly detaching from his body, hovering above it.

I feel him approach my world. He sees me clearly, intact, the way Tariq has seen me earlier. But unlike Tariq, Firas isn't scared. He knows he is drugged and doesn't think that what he sees is real. He thinks he is hallucinating. The tranquilizer has made him feel happy, but he's not happy to see me. He doesn't smile to me. He sulks and stares at me foolishly as if I'm the reason behind every foul circumstance he has had in his entire life.

He hears the sheikh asking him what his last wish is, and he hears himself asking for *kanefeh*. He says he wants

it from Habibaeh Sweets in downtown. The sheikh directs
the detective to bring *kanefeh* from Habibaeh Sweets in
downtown. He dictates the shahada to Firas and asks him to
pray.

When the *kanefeh* is brought, Firas eats it with no
appetite. He doesn't finish it. He is blindfolded and led to the
backyard where the gallows have been set. Two detectives hold
him, one from the right and one from the left, and steer him
toward the rope. I see everything clearly and I am gripped
by fear and worry more than Firas himself. But despite the
gravity of what's happening, I experience a strange shift.
Suddenly, it seems like the events in front of me are taking
place somewhere else. Firas approaching the hanging rope
feels no different than a man crossing the road to get to his
job, or a woman going up the escalator at the mall, or Tariq
sipping his morning coffee on the balcony of his house. Just
normal events, devoid of any real meaning.

As Firas approaches his ending, I realize the reason
behind my presence here. I haven't left Earth because I had to
wait for him. I'm still here because I had to welcome him and
accompany him on.

For the first time since my death, in this suspended space,
I feel heaviness settle on my soul. Or a mixture of awe and
anger for not belonging to either world.

'Why me?' I scream and try to escape and fly away. No
one replies.

I only manage to cover a few meters before I hit invisible
walls, as if the plaza in which Firas is about to be executed is
nothing but a cement room with four walls and a ceiling in a
parallel world. I calm down and start wondering. Why aren't
any of Firas's deceased uncles or grandparents sent to welcome
him instead of me? Does being connected to him in life mean
I have to be stuck with him in the hereafter? Is it possible that

our marriage contract is valid and binding even in death?

Was I supposed to divorce him before leaving my body in order not to be stuck with him in the hereafter? Does he realize that too? Or is he like Alice in Wonderland, floating in a soft world colored a rosy hue by the tranquilizer?

Firas hovers in between worlds. I feel a hand stretch out and touch me, as if there is someone who wants to diffuse the intensity of this moment and soften the impact of our meeting. Images of our beautiful memories start floating in front of us, tucked inside colorful air bubbles, each illuminated in turn, harmoniously and seamlessly taking us from one memory to another. Firas and I see them at the same time. Scenes from the past appear different from how I remember them. They document a happy ending to an ideal loving husband, not a miserable failure of a marriage. As if love stories have to always end in happily ever after, even if they are ugly stories unworthy of being told.

The biggest among those bubbles holds a memory from our wedding. It shows a panoramic shot of Firas and me raising the sword we grip in our hands to cut our wedding cake. We appear beautiful and elegant, smiling happily, slicing the wedding cake in unison. In reality, Firas was sour because I gripped the sword before he did. He hurried to tighten his grip on it and made sure he was in charge of slicing the cake, thinking it was the perfect way to reassert his manhood.

The following memory is edited just like the previous one. After cutting the cake, the guests demand in one voice, 'Kiss! Kiss! Kiss!" Firas and I lock lips like two lovers at the end of a Hollywood movie. The guests applaud us happily and celebrate our incredible love. But it was different on our actual wedding night. Firas and I felt shy and refused to oblige the guests. When they insisted, Firas hugged me and planted a kiss on my forehead instead of my lips.

After that kiss in the bubble, our wedding song, "The Republic of my Heart," plays. I am dancing to its lurid lyrics in front of Firas. Firas repeats the words. I shake my hips in my wedding dress and dance around my groom. He carries on, clapping, singing, deepening his voice:

> *Our daughters don't work with their certificates.*
> *Our daughters are spoiled*
> *Everything is at their service.*

I shake my hips more and continue dancing around him, ignoring the meaning of the lyrics. The wedding is perfect in the bubble. No conflict. No disagreement. I remember it differently though. I remember the feeling of goosebumps on my arms when I heard the song start. I had never liked that song because its lyrics were belittling and demeaning to women. I had asked Firas to tell the DJ not to play it on our wedding. The song angered me. I left Firas dancing by himself in the middle of the dance floor, shimmied my way to the DJ, and asked him to change the song right away. The DJ switched the song and plays Nancy Ajram's "I Might Fight with You But I'll Never Leave You." That song foreshadowed my life with Firas where arguments became the norm in the two years we lived together, augmented by our inability to leave each other.

The irony about this apparition of "The Republic of my Heart" is how the lyrics apply to him and not to me. He is the one who ends up sitting at home unemployed. He is the one who believes that despite being unemployed and lazy, he still has the right to be spoiled, every whim catered to.

In another bubble, Firas emerges out of the bathroom of our honeymoon suite in Phuket, Thailand. His chest is bare, a white towel wrapped around his hips. He approaches me to the tune of soft music playing in the background and I slide toward him smiling happily, my hair flowing as freely as the model in the Head and Shoulders commercial. I'm wearing a revealing nightgown showing my shoulders and part of my breasts. I gaze at his eyes, put my hand on his shoulder, and let him put his arms around my waist as we swoon together like Romeo and Juliet.

I loved Firas that day in Phuket. But the reality wasn't as perfect as it now appears in the bubble. We were both exhausted after a long 10-hour flight, including lengthy layovers at two airports. We reached the hotel at dawn and slept for barely three hours. When we woke up, Firas had a stomachache accompanied by a fever and severe diarrhea which didn't leave him for a few days. But, despite his miserable condition, he didn't want to disappoint his bride on the first day of the honeymoon. He took a quick shower right after waking up. He came out of the bathroom, arms tight around his chest, trying to stop himself from shivering. When he approached me and hugged me, I felt his rising fever. I put my palm on his forehead and felt his skin boiling, so I asked him to rest and put off sex until he felt better. I helped him lie in bed and called the doctor. When Firas's fever went down slightly, he tried again to be intimate because he felt guilty. I didn't stop him. We had lukewarm sex, the same as the night before. After that, his fever came back again.

And there he is now, in front of all those colorful bubbles, walking toward the gallows with a fever similar to the one he had on our honeymoon. He only sees me after the rope is slipped around his neck and the chair is knocked off from under his feet. His body shakes and hangs in the air as he fights to catch his last breath.

And then he is still, a lifeless corpse.

CHAPTER 18

GOODBYE MA'AM

TARIQ

TARIQ is shocked when he sees Firas's photo in the newspaper the next day, hanging from a rope at the Plaza. It is as if he hasn't realized that the death sentence against Firas was a real sentence and would be carried out sooner or later. Maybe he wished, somewhere deep inside him, that some kind of heavenly justice would intervene and miraculously save Firas, and that this would happen without him having to endanger his own life and confess to what happened. He has been living in an illusion, trying to convince himself that everything that has happened to him since my death is no more than a nightmare from which he will eventually wake up. Once that happens, things will go back to normal again.

But when Tariq unfolds the newspaper at his clinic, he feels a lump in his throat as he reads the headline: "DEATH SENTENCE CARRIED OUT ON SWEIFIEH CRIMINAL". That headline with bold letters on the first page jolts Tariq and confirms the reality to him. It is a clear statement telling him that even if he has had no hand in my death, he is now directly responsible for Firas losing his life. He feels as guilty as if he had hanged Firas himself.

Tariq hates himself. He can't stand the man he has become. It is too late now to reverse what has happened, but Tariq decides to go to the police to confess.

When Tariq tells the detective what happened, he doesn't cry, nor does he collapse or stutter. He narrates the entire story knowing that his decision to confess is irreversible. He doesn't allow himself to hesitate and doesn't let his feeling overpower him. He pauses briefly to catch his breath, forces himself to continue. He describes the sexual relationship we had together and the events of the day, with all the embarrassing details. Despite the disgusted and shocked expression on the face of the detective listening to him, he continues.

The detective lets Tariq finish his story without interrupting him. He seems bewildered, trying to figure out the best way to address the sudden catastrophe Tariq has thrown at him. On one hand, he believes that Tariq is telling the truth. On the other, the story sounds so strange and far-fetched that it requires careful examination to ascertain its details. But regardless of how strange the story is or whether Tariq is telling the truth not, whether Tariq is mentally stable or not (the detective certainly thinks he is not), it is self-evident that the detective has reached the scary conclusion the he himself is responsible for executing an innocent man. He clenches his fist tight and seems to be fighting a strong desire to stand up and punch Tariq hard to punish him for his stupidity.

The detective is fuming inwardly. How could Tariq remain quiet all that time only to come and confess today a few hours after Firas is executed? How dare he act so irresponsibly and get rid of my body in that way if he didn't have a hand in my death?

The detective curbs his anger and looks at Tariq's bent head. He puts his palm on his mouth and takes a deep breath, unsure of what to do. He has to evaluate his options: should he reopen the case, face fierce backlash for mishandling it earlier, and ultimately risk enraging the public? Or should he stand up for the truth, if the truth is indeed what Tariq has just told him, and let that sex story out in the open with its immodest details? What will that mean to him personally and professionally? How will he confront his bosses and explain to them the deadly mistake he has committed by accusing an innocent man? And what if Tariq's new information does not add up? Should he take a risk and reopen the case and risk committing other detrimental mistakes?

The detective goes over his options. He realizes that the best way to address the issue at hand is to force himself to believe Tariq's words, strange as they are. And that's why he decides, on a human not a professional impulse, and for the interest of everyone involved, not to reopen the case.

The detective seems eager for Tariq to leave quickly. He doesn't want to see him again. He has two options: either inform Tariq of his decision quietly and convince him to withdraw his confession, go back to his wife and kids and resume his life in a normal way as if nothing had happened; or force Tariq to withdraw his confession and never repeat what he said again by locking him up for a couple of days to teach him a lesson.

A person like him might lean toward the second option. Tariq might not be a criminal who deserves spend long years in jail or be executed, but he most certainly deserves to be punished for his cowardice and terrible actions in coming forward too late, after Firas is executed. But locking Tariq up for two days and beating him might leave visible marks on his body and alarm his family, who would in turn ask unwanted questions. That's why the detective decides to resort to another line of action.

He stands in front of his desk, approaches Tariq and pats him on the shoulder. 'Get up!' He says to Tariq. 'Go to your wife and kids and forget that you came here today.'

Tariq stares in shock at the detective, who adds harshly, 'I don't want to see your face after today. If I ever see you again, I swear to God I'll finish you off with my own hands.'

Tariq can't believe himself. He is about to object. After

all, he is there because his feelings of guilt toward Firas have tormented him. He has come forward because he loathes the image of the coward he has become. But the detective letting him off the hook proves to him that his actions may have not been as bad as he thought. There is now another person carrying the heavy burden of that guilt with him. Tariq realizes that the punishment he deserves might not be proportional to the punishment he would receive if he insists that the detective reopens the case. With the pardon he has just received in the form of the detective's dismissal, he is protecting his family from the injustice they would have been subjected to because of him. He can now shield his children from an unnecessary scandal they had no hand in creating.

His courage fails him one more time. He tries to speak, but his tongue refuses to move. He realizes that he has to remain quiet if he wants to save his life. The case is closed and the detective has given him another chance at life which he should not throw away. In the eyes of everyone, he will remain the way he has always been – Dr. Tariq, heart surgeon, a respected man with high social standing who is admired and valued by many. And why not? He is indeed a respectable man. He is not a thief nor is he a criminal. He fulfills his social duties perfectly well, perhaps much more so than many other men. He hasn't killed anyone. In fact, he has saved hundreds of lives. The number of surgeries he has performed is endless and the number of hearts he has filled with happiness by saving the lives of their beloved ones is limitless.

He has slipped in a moment of weakness, the way I slipped when I hesitated in divorcing Firas. The way Firas slipped in insisting to hold on to me despite the failure of our marriage. Who among us is not affected by moments of weakness? If Firas and I did not get the chance, why can't Tariq have it?

I watch Tariq leave the police station and head to his car seemingly lost. He doesn't seem happy or afraid. He unlocks his car and sits behind the steering wheel. He gazes at the horizon and sees my face form in the clouds.

He remembers the first time we met at the door of his clinic and wishes that time would go back so he could kiss my hand and hug me. He wishes he could hold on to those beautiful moments which united us. If he could rewind time, he would have listened to me and agreed with me when I got so worked up and decided to tell Firas about our relationship. I didn't care back then and I wanted Firas out of the way. Keeping my relationship from Tariq a secret made me feel I was doing something wrong, as though I was actually cheating on Firas and was too embarrassed to admit to that. But I wasn't cheating on him and I didn't feel like I was doing something wrong. I only met Tariq after I lost all hope of fixing my relationship with Firas. I stayed with Firas just to keep up appearances, no more and no less. He begged me and pressured me to stay. I kept my relationship with Tariq a secret out of respect for him and his family. We had agreed to keep it a secret until we had a chance to split from our spouses, but time betrayed us and tested Tariq's courage again in a way that jeopardized his future.

This experience might teach him something about making the right decision in the future.

Tariq looks at my image in the clouds and sees me wave goodbye at him. I see his tears fall. He sighs and wipes them as he starts his car and heads back to Ikram.

The End